Fortune Smiles as Love Divides

MARGARET NYHON

Published by Willow Press

Author contact: margaretf@hotmail.co.nz

A catalogue record for this book is available from the National Library of New Zealand.

ISBN 978-0-473-67742-8 (paperback)

ISBN 978-0-473-67743-5 (EPUB)

Contents

1. The rapid climb — 1
2. Reece — 7
3. Kennedy — 19
4. Lincoln — 29
5. Six months on — 37
6. The new arrival — 57
7. The seeking begins — 71
8. The investment world — 97
9. A stranger calls — 103
10. A shock revelation — 119
11. Cryptocurrency makes headlines — 133
12. The divided family — 143
13. Drifting apart — 161
14. Moving up the ladder at work — 191
15. The surprise visit — 203
16. Life without Reece — 223
17. The meeting — 233
18. Virtual reality versus the real world — 237
19. Lily's dream — 249

Also by Margaret Nyhon — 253
About the Author — 255

The crypto and virtual reality worlds were once just a dream,
But in the end, will they reign supreme?
More people today are working from their homes,
So on their computers and gaming devices, they work and play
alone.

The rapid climb

Now that the three young men had made an entry into the crypto world of secrecy and concealment, it was time for them to celebrate. No more worries of having to send money around the world through the banking systems; that era was done and dusted. Now they could move currencies worldwide by the electronic system, based on cryptographic proof, instead of trust. This system guaranteed them full anonymity, but with this came risks. It is speculative and volatile and can be subject to boom-and-bust cycles. But at this moment in time, it was a boom cycle, so they had captured the crest of the wave and were well on their way to become billionaires. Cryptocurrencies were the up-and-coming way to operate in the world of big finance.

Lincoln, Kennedy and Reece started buying bitcoin before it rose dramatically in value. It was the dream of these three lads to catch a rising market; that would make them rich. They bought their first bitcoins for $150 a coin, which had now increased in value to $62,000 per coin. Because its supply is limited to 21 million coins, there was only one way it was going and that was upwards, as institutional investors saw it as an escape from vulnerability and inflation. The lads had spent many hours poring over what was the right investment to make a quick buck.

Lincoln, being the computer nerd, sorted all the information he needed online, but it was Kennedy who had the business head, who followed what was cool in today's markets. Without the back-up of Reece's money, the other two lads were going nowhere. It was brain power versus financial power that drew them together as a successful team.

Friday night was booked in as boys' night at Lincoln's bachelor pad, as this was where all the problem solving was done, not that there were problems any more. They had all disappeared when bitcoin took its massive hike. Reece's family inheritance was a welcome relief to a somewhat ailing threesome, who had up until now made several 'bum' investments, costing Lincoln and Kennedy the little savings they had. The inheritance was what started them on the right path, as they had studied cryptocurrency and decided this was the right move and the right time. It was relatively new and was a gamble, but they were young, vibrant and smart and this ticked all the right boxes. Kennedy had read it was similar to gold, both having the same value. After all, he was the whizz kid on financial matters.

All three needed each other, as their fields combined gave them a huge advantage. Lincoln's computer expertise was a leading component, as he had to be able to convert ordinary plain text into unintelligent text and vice versa. Cryptography converts data into formula, only able to be read by the persons involved, preventing third parties or the public from gathering any information. No one owns this network, but anyone with a link can contribute to it. For a person to obtain a 'block' it has to be with the approval of the majority of bitcoin holders.

Their backgrounds were entirely different. They had only met while in their last year at university, as they were in separate flatting situations. It was a common goal that brought them together and that was money. They had big dreams for the future, and the opposite sex were excluded. Front and centre was to be rich; the girls would follow.

At the beginning, no one wanted the currency to be touched; it was to be left there, so they could keep tabs on its growth. Their cryptocurrency portfolio was very healthy indeed, and with each week that the growth continued, so did their excitement. They had passed the millionaire status and were now teetering on the brink of becoming billionaires. From the sale of Reece's parents' property, they were able to buy a modest bachelor pad each so they could have their independence. They felt that now their fortunes had changed, living 24/7 in each other's company was not for them, and they did not want to chance a fallout among friends. Besides, their sexual desires were stirring, so they needed their own space, girls being back on their agenda.

Kennedy was the playboy. Several females had come on to him, but he had resisted, leaving them broken-hearted, this being his ploy: love them and leave them! Not that he had loved anyone at this stage; he just had not met the right girl that was as intelligent as him. There were plenty of ordinary girls out there, but he was saving himself for the right one, the smart one who would challenge him at his own game! Was he being truthful or would he be burnt? This he was about to experience!

At the university they held quiz nights that the three friends attended regularly. Although they had finished their education, as past students they were allowed to use the university facilities. They teamed up together, but each night they had to find someone to join them to form a team of four persons. Tonight, a stranger was looking to become a team member, so Reece signalled for her to come to their table and join them. Kennedy was a bit annoyed, as he had spotted talent elsewhere, but it was too late.

The stranger introduced herself as Lily and said she was in her fourth year of study, to become a lawyer. Her appearance was that of a student, her hair was tied up and she wore a beret. This did nothing for Kennedy, who was not amused, although he did pick up on the fact she was studying to become a lawyer, so perhaps she did have a bit of intelligence.

It wasn't until the quiz started that the intelligence came out in the open. Lily knew all the answers, several that Kennedy did not know. How could such a plain-looking person be so bright, he asked himself. Did he think she was worthy of a bit more attention? But it was too late, as Reece had commandeered her.

When the quiz papers were handed in to be marked, the winners were announced. "Could someone from the team 'three-plus-one' come forward and claim their prize money?" Kennedy stood up, but Reece asked him to sit down. "Lily answered all the questions correctly so she will represent us." This was a slap in the face for Kennedy for this person was a total stranger.

With this Lily protested, but Reece persuaded her to represent them. As she collected the prize money, the quizmaster said to her, "Very good, your team answered all the questions correctly. What do you do?" Lily told him she was studying to be a lawyer, then she would like to work her way to the position of a high court judge. "Good luck young lady," he said. All the quiz participants clapped as she walked back to their table. Suddenly, because all the limelight was on this girl, something stirred in Kennedy's belly. As she was about to be seated, Reece stood up and asked her to accompany him to the bar, as he wanted to shout her a drink.

This was the last Kennedy saw of her that night, but not the last time he thought about her, as he had a sleepless night. The mere thought of her answering all the questions baffled him, as she was a nobody really. He thought that she must have a few brains to become a lawyer, but was he trying to reconcile the fact that here was someone as intelligent as himself? He didn't like this feeling, it left him baffled.

During the week, the lads went back to their full-time employment. Kennedy worked for a high-profile company as a financial advisor. Lincoln was employed as a computer programmer for a company, programming new games. He'd been head-hunted for the job. Reece was the less intelligent one of them; he was a hotel manager. His parents were both in the medical profession, his father a surgeon and his mother a phycologist. He was an only child but did not inherit their intelligence, something which upset him.

Reece

Reece had a loving upbringing and as an only child he was doted on. He had a private nanny as his parents both worked full-time, but any spare time, they spent with him. He was taken on holidays all around the world, and money was never a problem. He felt at times he never quite lived up to his parents' expectations, but this was only in his own mind. He was of average intelligence, never achieving high marks at school, but he was popular with his peers. His personality was his main attribute. When he left college, he was offered a job at a posh hotel as a bell-boy. The hotel was owned by a family friend who could see potential in this outgoing young man, but he had to start at the bottom and work his way up. It didn't take long before he was on front reception. He had a knack of remembering people's names and this was important in the hospitality industry, as it made guests feel important or special. The hotel owner received many accolades from guests about Reece, thus pushing him higher up the ladder.

His boss offered to pay for him to go to university to do a hospitality course, so in time he could become hotel management material. This course would take two years, and in the holidays, he was expected to come back to the hotel and work. Nearing the end of his two-year course, his parents were on holiday in Australia, when the unthinkable happened. He received a phone call from his aunty in Alice Springs, to say his parents had died in a light plane crash. They had been holidaying around Australia with his aunt and uncle, his mother's sister and her husband. The four of them had driven up to Alice Springs. While there, Reece's mother wanted to see Uluru from the air, so they hired a light aircraft to take them for a scenic flight.

Only his parents and the pilot took the flight and when the plane was overdue, fear started to mount. Had something happened? It was only when they saw the authorities coming towards them, that they knew the news was not going to be what they wanted to hear. The plane had crashed and burst into flames on impact. All that was left was charred remains of both plane and passengers.

The uncle and aunt were beside themselves. Reece would be devastated. On learning what had happened, he burst into tears.

"Please Reece, catch the next flight to Brisbane then a connecting flight to Alice Springs. We will stay here until you arrive, as we want to know the cause of the accident," said a heartbroken aunt. Reece was shattered, as he was very close to his parents, being their only child and had never thought about life without them. On compassionate grounds he was able to catch the next flight to Australia, and the airlines would try to arrange for him to get a seat on a connecting flight to Alice Springs. He rung his friends to let them know what had happened, as they had spent time with his parents. They offered their condolences as this was a shock to them as well.

As the plane touched down in Alice Springs and taxied to the terminal, he could see his relatives standing on the top tier of the terminal building. He had silently wept all the way after leaving Brisbane and it seemed like a lifetime had passed as he thought of his parents' terrible death. He walked out into the arrival area and there stood his remaining family; the tears were still there as they embraced each other in silent grief. No one spoke, the heartache they were suffering was still raw.

Reece was the first to speak, "What happened?" were the only audible words he could mutter.

"We were waiting for your mother and father to return when we received the terrible news. We did not know what to do. Their bodies are still out there and cannot be removed until the air accident authorities investigate," his aunt told him.

This was the last straw for Reece, and he broke down as he thought of his parents still lying at the scene of the crash.

"Come, Reece, let's go for a coffee," suggested his uncle as he led them to a café in the airport.

The next morning as Reece woke, his head was still reeling, he could not even remember going to bed, everything was a blur. He supposed this was the very room his parents had slept in, the night before last, as they were sharing a unit with his uncle and aunt.

After breakfast the three of them headed off to the airport to await news of the recovery of the bodies. They were not allowed to visit the crash site; there was nothing to see, as all that was left was charred remains. His parents would have to identified by forensic investigators by dental records. This would mean a wait of several days.

The next thing to think about was the funeral: what would they do and where? His aunt suggested they hold a private funeral in Alice Springs, then he could take their ashes back to New Zealand. This seemed to make sense to Reece, as he was still numb from this shocking loss. He just couldn't think of not ever seeing his parents again.

"You know your parents loved you dearly, Reece. You were just like their own son."

"What do you mean? I was their son?" he answered. It was at that moment the aunt realised that Reece hadn't been told he was adopted, and now it was too late to retract her words.

"Your parents could not have children of their own so adopted you as a baby. Did they not tell you? Oh Reece, I am so sorry that you had to learn this from me."

He could not answer, as the bad news just kept coming. He had so much to take on board, but to find out he was adopted, what a shock! His first reaction was,

"Why didn't they tell me?" Now it was too late to ask them questions.

The following day they had arranged to meet up with the company whose aircraft his parents flew with. The company manager was most upset and asked Reece to sit down so they could talk. He asked him when he was leaving Alice Springs. Reece wanted to leave as soon as everything was sorted out.

"The company would like to offer you a one-off payment of $250,000 as compensation for your loss," he said to Reece, hoping he would accept, and this would be the end of the matter. The last thing on his mind was a payment for the loss of his parents, as what he wanted to know was how the accident happened. Was it pilot error or was it a maintenance shortfall? The manager told them the authorities were still investigating. It was then his uncle intervened and told Reece not to accept the offer until they found the cause, so he took his uncle's advice.

Reece was now back in New Zealand living in his parents' home. He had so many things to sort out, as he had no idea of his family's financial affairs. He was in his last semester before finishing his hospitality course, so he had moved out of his shared flat. His flatmate friends, Lincoln and Kennedy, were very supportive, as they could see he was struggling to cope with his parents' death. Reece had not mention to anyone about his adoption as he was still processing this. When the family solicitor call Reece into his office, he was shocked to learn how much money was now his, as his parents had life insurances, work superannuation and a new offer had come through from the sightseeing plane company of $500,000.

He was now a very wealthy young man, not that he had thought about the money side of things, as he was still grieving. The results had come through on the cause of the crash. It appeared that the plane was three months overdue for its maintenance check, and therefore it was due to the company's negligence. No wonder a higher offer had been made to him. They were admitting liability and did not want Reece to take them to court, as a court case could go on for years, at God knows what cost. To Reece the damage was done, he had lost his parents and no amount of money could compensate for this!

He wanted it all to end, as now he had the property to sell. He felt so alone in the big house, there was no love there any more, and it felt hollow and empty. It did not take long to sell as it was prime real estate. The section could be subdivided and several flats could be built on the site. Now Reece could move back in with his flatmates, Lincoln and Kennedy. Here began the fortunes of the three young men. First, a moderate bachelor pad of their own, then their entry into the crypto world.

Today Reece had planned to meet Lily and take her out for dinner. He had taken her home after the quiz and she had asked him in for a coffee. They had an enjoyable time, talk flowed easy and there was plenty of laughter. Reece felt reasonably comfortable in her company, although she was definitely an intellect. He had some doubts, as he felt he did not match her intelligence, but she seemed to like him, otherwise perhaps she wouldn't have accepted his offer to go to dinner. He thought she would be a perfect match for Kennedy, but unbeknown to him she had other ideas. Lily thought Kennedy was a pompous 'prick'; he was not her type of guy. Since Reece found out about his adoption, he now knew why he wasn't as smart as his mother and father. He wasn't their birth son, but who was he? He had no leads, but now he had more important things on his mind … Lily and money. Through the week Kennedy had kept on his case, asking about his association with Lily and whether he fancied her, which of course he did.

When Reece arrived at Lily's flat, she was waiting for him at the gate. He arrived in his father's Jaguar as he couldn't bring himself to sell it; he knew how much it had meant to him. This was a little part of him he had left.

Reece got the shock of his life, as standing at the gate was a goddess, her hair hung down around her shoulders and her fitting dress showed off her body contour. She looked exquisite. A quick thought flashed through his mind. Yes, she was definitely Kennedy material; would he have to fight to hold on to her? He knew Kennedy was a smooth operator.

Reece opened the car door for her and saw she was comfortably seated. This didn't go unnoticed by Lily; he seemed a right gentleman. He asked if she had somewhere special that she would like to dine, but she was happy to leave it up to him. He took her to his favourite restaurant, where they had nice food and an enjoyable night.

On their way home Reece stopped off at Kennedy's

pad just to let him see what a lovely girl Lily really was, and he wanted to show her off! As they entered, they were met by wolf-whistles from Lincoln who was also visiting, but Kennedy's eyes were fixed on the vision before him. He could not believe this was their quiz partner, the one with a ponytail and the silly beret. He now wished he had first dibs on her, but was it too late?

Reece went to the kitchen and put the kettle on for them all to have a coffee. Lily was seated on the settee, and next thing Kennedy made his move and sat beside her, real close. Lily was right on to him and removed herself to help Reece in the kitchen. Kennedy's ego was dented, but his opinion of himself never waned, and his time would come. She would fall for him; it was only a matter of time.

The next time they all met was the following week at the university quiz. The three lads were waiting for Lily to arrive and she didn't disappoint, although to Kennedy's disappointment, she had her hair in a ponytail and was wearing her beret, which he thought was degrading. But Reece liked her this way; this was just who she was.

Once the quiz got underway and the questions were forthcoming, there was a slight difference of opinion between Kennedy and Lily on two of the answers. He thought he was right, but Lily knew otherwise and his bolshiness annoyed her, so she let him make the final choice. There was a distinct rivalry between these two.

After the papers were gathered up and collected to be marked, they waited patiently for their name to be announced as the winners, all except Lily. The winners were announced and they came second, with two wrong answers. When Reece checked the papers, the two wrong answers were the ones Lily wanted to change, so he drew Kennedy's attention to this, but he just took it on the chin, as if it was of no significance. He was a hard nut to crack, but to be humbled by a female, inwardly he was seething. Why, he asked himself, did he feel like this? She was a nobody really, and he could do better than that. There were plenty of beautiful girls out there who would be grateful to be asked out on a date.

On leaving the quiz, Reece drove Lily to her flat where they sat in the car and talked. He wanted to lean over and kiss her, as his feelings were growing towards her, but then he thought, perhaps it would be easier for this to happen when he opened the car door, as he would be closer to her. As he helped her out, he held her in his arms and gently kissed her cheek, and this soon developed into a full passionate session. Lily was a willing participant as she had secretly hoped he would make a move. They found it hard to break from each other, but Reece made the first move for fear his hands would start wandering. He didn't want to jeopardise their friendship, and he had to control his testosterone rush. It was too soon to expect more from her.

Today Reece was back at work at his hotel. His boss, who was a family friend, had given him six weeks' leave so he could settle his parents' estate and pick himself up from his sudden loss. Lily had helped him mend. He told her what had happened to his family and that it was still raw in his heart. The staff were happy to have him back as they missed his jovial ways. He was well liked by everyone, particularly the female staff, but hotel policy did not allow him to date any staff member. Not that this worried him, as he had a girlfriend who had captured his heart. His two-year hospitality course at university had benefitted him, as he had been promoted from duty manager to manager. He felt proud that he was now in a position of trust, and he felt deep down he was moving towards Lincoln and Kennedy's level.

Today was Friday, the boys' night at Lincoln's pad, as they wanted to see the balance in their 'wallet'. It had been a big decision to venture into cryptocurrency. Lincoln, being the computer whizz, knew that he had to deposit cash into their account to be able to purchase cryptocurrency, the value being based on the current exchange rate, and then their purchase would be held in their wallet. To view their cryptocurrency balance, all they had to do was check the amount that was sitting in their wallet. To keep the wallet secure they had to make sure that when they verified their cryptocurrency balance, they only use the public address from their portfolio. The public address for each currency is the string of characters shown after your address, under the currency heading.

Only a competent computer user, who understands the digital medium, can successfully operate in the crypto world. It is a fast-paced world and most beginner investors become excited and get caught up in the hype. Cryptocurrency is a digital medium of exchanging goods and services based on a publicly accessible ledger in a secure system. The governments and banks do not control it; instead it is owned and controlled by everyone in the system.

To verify cryptocurrency transactions, a process known as crypto-mining must be conducted. Mining is a very energy-intensive process and requires enormous computing power and complex algorithms – logical arithmetical procedures for solving problems – in order to be successful. Thus, Lincoln was their man. The other two had to rely on his honesty and judgement, to run the technical side of things.

The lads had to choose which cryptocurrency was the safest, as they were amazed to find there were more than 5000 in existence, so they decided to go with bitcoin, as it seemed to be the best known. Bitcoin works the opposite way to traditional currency, as there is no control over it. Being young and up to date with get-rich-quick schemes, they realised cryptocurrency was the biggest revolution in the finance industry, in the last few decades. It was created to underwrite the banking system, to break free from governments and banks and central control of the world's money. Investors were sick of banks devaluing money and the rising inflation and saw cryptocurrency as a means of beating the system and taking away their power.

On visiting their wallet, Lincoln found their cryptocurrency had fallen in value, not a lot, but nevertheless it was a correction which left him a little on edge. But they knew it could fluctuate either way, as this was how it worked. They were along for the ride and had to deal with the vulnerability that would face them on this journey.

"Guess what boys, we haven't made the billionaire status yet. We have dropped a good few thousand dollars, but it will rise again, it's not over yet!" he declared. What was a few thousand dollars when they were dealing in millions? Kennedy was not at all worried, as being a financial advisor, he knew vulnerability was how the world worked, especially in today's environment. Nothing was stable, things changed with each hour, and they knew this came with risks. Taking a risk was how one climbed the ladder to success, as success was not luck, it was taking opportunities when they arrived … and that was now!

Kennedy

Kennedy's life was not an easy ride. His mother and father were high-school sweethearts, but their relationship was volatile. They met at high school and fell head over heels in love. Their school days were fun filled and this was the place where you met up with the opposite sex and indulged with different partners, but not Kennedy's parents, as they had each other. When they finished their schooling, his mother got a job in a local department store and his father took on a butcher's apprenticeship. They were saving for a deposit for their own home.

One day a stranger came to town and took up a job in the department store. This was when their relationship ended, as Kennedy's mother was smitten by this newcomer. She suddenly felt she had missed out on chances in life. Thus, the start of a stormy affair with the stranger, and she had never known such excitement, but she soon realised that excitement could end as quick as it started, as she was dropped. He had moved on to someone else. At this stage she disappeared off the radar for several months. When she returned, she went back to her childhood sweetheart. He was not as exciting as her fling, but he was reliable.

They married and twelve months later Kennedy was born. His mother was not happy just being a housewife, as she missed the excitement she had tasted, so she sought a friendship outside her marriage. When she realised she was pregnant again, she didn't know who the father of the baby was. This was her secret and would remain so. With two little ones to look after, her days were filled, so she settled down, not wanting to make another mistake!

Life carried on in a mundane fashion, but she was not happy and this took its toll on their marriage. Suddenly one day she announced she was leaving; she had met someone else, and that was the last the children saw of their mother. Their father brought up Kennedy and his sister. He was a good man and did his best for his children.

Was Kennedy's high opinion of himself the result of his broken home life? He always had it in his head he would be among the high flyers one day, and it was a dream he hoped to bring to reality. So, finance was where he had to start. His father worked long hours to pay for him and his sister to go to university, for which he was grateful and made a promise to himself that he would look after him in later life. He never saw his mother again and this left him feeling a little distrust for the opposite sex; he felt they were lesser beings than a man. His luck was in his looks as he was tall, dark and handsome, and he knew it. But he put all his spare time into his study so he could achieve high marks so when he qualified, he could get a good job with a reputable finance company. This is exactly what happened!

Now he was flatting with Lincoln and Reece. They were waiting on the sale of Reece's parents' home, then they were going to buy a modest bachelor pad each. He was extremely grateful to Reece, as without his parents' money they would not be in the cryptocurrency world, among the high flyers.

Now that the lads were settled in their respective homes, Kennedy was on the lookout for a bit of fun involving the opposite sex. For several years he had shunned any females that showed an interest in him, as he had to establish himself among the upper class, which was his ultimate goal. Girls were not part of his get-rich scheme, but now the time had come to have some fun. But this did not come without its problems. The girl he couldn't get out of his mind belonged to Reece. He tried to convince himself she was a nobody, but this didn't stack up, as she was a very intelligent young lady, in fact a perfect match for him. He could not understand why she settled for Reece as he was just a hotel manager, especially when she could have him. Fancy ladies were his for the picking, and he had even tried dating ladies older than himself, hoping to find the perfect match intelligent wise, but no one came near Lily's standard. He had even forgiven her for wearing that stupid beret to the university quiz nights; it was what lay beneath her student cladding that excited him.

It all happened the night Reece brought Lily around to his apartment on the way home from their date. She looked exquisite, and he had even tried to get close to her while she was on his settee, but she rejected him by moving out to the kitchen to be with Reece. He was waiting for the day when she would get over Reece and come to him. In the meantime, he would carry on having fun; his love-them-and-leave-them attitude would suffice for the time being.

One night the boys arranged to each bring a friend along for a night out, first dinner, then the casino. Kennedy knew he had to find the 'standout jewel'; he would show them all what a real lady looked like! They had arranged to meet at the Laguna restaurant at 7 o'clock. Reece and Lily were the first to arrive, followed by Lincoln and his partner who all knew each other. Then all eyes turned to Kennedy, for on his arm was the most beautiful blonde dressed in a glamorous gown that left nothing to the imagination.

"Hi everyone, this is Marcia, she owns a beauty parlour," announced a pompous Kennedy. Everyone was polite, even a little stunned by this fabulous creature in their midst. As soon as she opened her mouth, however, her true self was revealed.

"Hello everyone, Kennedy and I are very good friends,

and we both love the social life. All my friends are in the fashion industry, hence my lovely gown. We are a great match, aren't we, honey?"

Lily smiled to herself, thinking: you might have the most glamorous partner, but also the most empty-headed one. As they gathered around the table to dine, Reece pulled a chair out for Lily to be seated, as did Lincoln for his partner, but not Kennedy, who sat down first and tapped the chair next to him for Marcia to sit on. Kennedy was seated directly opposite Lily. As conversation began, Lily remained quiet, as Marcia held the floor. She told of her overseas trips, her buying sprees and who she was acquainted with, which turned into a name-dropping session. Then she turned to Lily, "You are very quiet, Lily, what do you do?" Lily told her she was studying to be a lawyer, but before she finished, Marcia interrupted, "No wonder you're silent. What a boring life!"

Kennedy was annoyed that Marcia had cut Lily down so tried to make amends. "You're looking nice tonight, Lily. I like the flower in your hair, it really suits you," he told her.

"Thank you, Kennedy, Reece bought this especially for me tonight. I was really thrilled; he is so thoughtful," and with this she leaned over and kissed him.

This hurt Kennedy; he wished it was him she was kissing. Trust Reece to do the right thing and win the accolades.

Next it was on to the casino. On their arrival they gathered for a cocktail before hitting the gambling tables. Kennedy wanted to apologise to Lily for Marcia's impertinent remark about her boring profession. He had his moment when he saw Reece heading to the bathroom. "I'm sorry for what Marcia said to you earlier. I think you are amazing," he whispered. This took Lily completely by surprise: fancy Kennedy apologising, not for himself but his girlfriend!

"You don't have to be sorry; I have met girls like Marcia before. They have it all on the outside but inwardly they are shallow, and they have never experienced happiness. All they want in life is to be noticed. She reminds me of someone I know," and with this she walked away.

Kennedy took a moment to digest what Lily had said. Yes, she was right about Marcia, she was an empty-headed show pony, but who was the other person she was referring to? He could not fathom that one out. While he was consuming his cocktail, he couldn't take his eyes off Lily. There were no 'airs and graces' about her and the flower in her hair looked perfect. He could imagine her on an exotic island swaying to the island music while encased in his arms, with his body pressed close to hers. Suddenly his dream was broken, and he was being dragged away by Marcia who was ready to gamble.

The party split and they all went their separate ways. Reece took Lily to the roulette wheel where they each placed a chip on their favourite number. Lily chose number 17 and Reece chose 26. The wheel spun and stopped on number 17, which meant Lily collected thirty-four chips. It was Lily's night as her pile of chips grew, but she still only played the one chip each game. Meanwhile

Kennedy and Marcia were playing ten chips each on a spin of the wheel as they both wanted to make big money, but they soon found out they could lose big money just as quick. After an hour they were totally broke so they looked for Reece and Lily to see how they were going. When they found them, they could not believe the pile of chips in front of Lily.

"Why are you only playing one chip?" asked Marcia.

Lily said she was cautious.

"Gosh, Kennedy and I played ten chips each game; it's more exciting."

"I'm happy with my one chip. Did you make ten times more than me?" Lily asked.

"No, we have lost our money, and we are going to leave now, aren't we Kennedy?"

"No, let's wait for a while and watch Lily play her one chip," said Kennedy.

"No, I am ready to go now," she sulked and walked off.

Kennedy apologised and hurriedly caught up with Marcia. "You were rude to my friends. I won't stand for that," he told her.

"I don't like that, Lily. She is 'miss goody two shoes', she's not my type. Why did you tell her she looked nice? You never told me that. I think you have the hots for her," she spat out to Kennedy. He never answered her, and the sooner he was rid of her the better.

The next time the team met was at the university quiz. Now Reece would stop off and pick Lily up on his way and bring her with him. She had ditched her beret, as she wasn't walking any more, so she let her auburn hair fall snugly around her shoulders. The student image was slowly disappearing, and she was embracing a new life, as now she and Reece were serious about each other. Lily had never met such a caring man; he was respectful, which is what she loved most about him. He treated her like a lady. Not like Kennedy; his girlfriends were just commodities that he used and discarded. Lily only tolerated him because of the close friendship the three boys had.

As they were seated before the quiz began, Lily couldn't help herself. "Wow, what a date Marcia was. I thought the two of you looked so good together, like two social butterflies. I bet she is your type of girl, so vivacious and out there, a little like yourself really?" She waited for his reply.

"I'm upset you think of me like that, Lily. She turned out to be a scatterbrain, and I'm not at all like her." This statement brought a smile to Lily's face, as he just never seemed to get what she was trying to tell him.

Kennedy noticed her smile and felt angry. Was she taking the mickey out of him? Couldn't she see that she was tormenting him, and that he was seething deep down inside? One day he would get even!

Silence was called for as the quiz began. Tonight, they wanted to win, not be second like last week. As the questions were being called out, as usual there were queries on several of the answers. Kennedy wanted to take charge, but the other team members sided with Lily, especially after last week. Bitterness was building inside of Kennedy, as once again she was showing him up, but only in his own mind. The hurt went beyond the quiz questions. He had feelings for Lily, but he was not getting any feedback from her. Well, not the feedback he expected, or wanted. Couldn't she see he wanted her for himself? As the quiz ended, he took the papers up to be marked. They ordered a drink while waiting for the results and it was then he noticed Lily's hand on Reece's knee. A thought flashed through his mind: why couldn't it have been him who felt the closeness displayed by Lily? Then came the all-important announcement, "Could the lovely young lady from team 'three plus one' come up and collect their prize money?"

"I'll go," announced Kennedy, but he was soon put in his place by Lincoln.

"No, Lily will collect the prize money. The quiz master asked her to come up." This was the final straw for Kennedy, again he was being overshadowed by his arch-rival. His mixed emotions were unsettling him. Was it love or hate? This was all new, and he felt lost, as for the first time in his life he had lost control, and this did not sit well with him.

As Lily collected their prize the crowd clapped and wolf-whistled at her, as she made her way back to their table. Reece stood up and put his arms around her and kissed her on her cheek, then Lincoln came over and shook her hand. Kennedy so wanted to hug her, and this he did. As his arms folded around her, he felt her warmth, which transferred from her body to his, sending sexual feelings to all the right places. This was a first, never had he felt this intense rush of love, and now he was convinced more than ever she belonged to him. "You have made us proud," he whispered in her ear. Lily couldn't wait to break from his hug, as he left her feeling cold and a little threatened. Thank goodness Lincoln was a nice decent guy; she felt safe with him.

Lincoln

Lincoln's life from a young age was centred around computers. His father owned a company that imported computers from all around the world, so there was always access to them. His mother was a wages clerk who worked for a local accounting firm, so she was also computer savvy. He had three siblings, two sisters and a brother, with Lincoln being the eldest. The children had the latest in Xbox games; anything electronic was available in their home. Lincoln knew right from a little boy where his future was going to take him. He learnt from a young age how to set up all types of computers. He could follow instructions and understood the tech jargon, so when it came to being taught at school, he knew more than the teachers. If any problems arose, they knew who to call upon … reliable Lincoln.

He wasn't much interested in other subjects as his brain was wired to the technology world. He excelled in this subject as well as maths. He failed in his other subjects but his knowledge in the computer and maths departments managed to gain him an entry into university. He wanted to do computer programming as he understood algorithms, which he had been using to accomplish the specific tasks needed, for the past couple of years. He had started to write his own scripts to build software, and all he needed to do now was package it and find a company that would release it.

Although computers can do amazing things, it cannot happen without a programmer, who tells it to behave in specific ways. He knew more than most, so he was the ideal man for the lads' entry into the world of cryptocurrency.

Lincoln's parents were proud of their son, although there were moments of opposition, when they tried to get him outdoors playing sport, but they didn't make much progress in this field. He was not a sports person, and to him it was a waste of energy; he had much more important things to do on his computer.

His siblings were upset when he went flatting, as he was their backstop with homework. He enjoyed helping them, but now it was time to move on, and he needed his own space. Besides, he now had met new friends at university. Lincoln was head-hunted by a tech company who heard of his exceptional computer skills, as well as building his own software. He was offered an unbelievable salary, one he thought was way out of his league, but his employers were only too happy to offer him this package, as he was an asset to them. They could see there was money to be made by this young man, as for his age, he had an exceptional grip on the technology world. Lincoln lived and breathed technology, there was so much more out there for him to discover; the world was his oyster. When the lads decided to investigate the world of cryptocurrency, they could not have found a better partner than Lincoln, and his savviness was their salvation.

This was where he met his current girlfriend. The company's receptionist took a shine to him when he first came to work for them. This only left Kennedy without a current girlfriend, but on the outside, he seemed happy to be playing the field. Little did his partners know the agony he was suffering when he saw Reece and Lily together. There was a cauldron boiling away, and not even he knew how it was all going to end.

Today Kennedy had received an e-mail from an IT company called Kaseya, who promised to help cryptocurrency investors. They were offering powerful security and IT management tools that were efficient, cost effective as well as secure. He decided to call a meeting as he wanted Lincoln's take on this company. He thought perhaps they should opt to go with them, as a safe back-up for their investment. This company had put out remote-management software to monitor and manage computers.

Kennedy wanted to be convinced they could manage it themselves, without the backup of Kaseya. He had read about ransomware attacks, where data is encrypted and the culprits demand payment in cryptocurrency in return for a key to decrypt the hostage data. This cybercrime was on the rise. Here lay Kennedy's concern, as he worried they might be targeted, so this meeting was to talk things through. The digital world, like the real world, would always have an element of criminality. Cybercrime is unable to be eliminated from the internet, just as there is crime in the physical world. Kennedy's biggest worry with cryptocurrency was that since there were no help desks, if you lost your wallet your money would be gone for good! It is not traceable.

With the arrival of Lincoln and Reece at Kennedy's pad, they could begin their meeting. Lincoln asked Kennedy what the purpose of the meeting was.

"I'm worried about ransomware attacks. Are you sure we are protected? I had an e-mail from a company who gave assurance that their remote-management software was secure, as they have big investors signed up with them. I want your input on this Lincoln."

Lincoln was a little surprised that Kennedy perhaps thought he did not have their investment under control. He answered straight back, "I am not in favour of a strange company taking control of our currency. I am savvy enough to know that it is safe in the wallet, as only I have the public address of our portfolio. If I keep this to myself, then no one can hijack our wallet. What do you think Reece? We have only been able to enter the crypto world because of your parents' estate. I want your thoughts on what we should do."

Reece trusted Lincoln completely, as he knew the lengths the company went to, to secure his expertise. "I will go along with you Lincoln. I don't think we need a company controlling our investment, and I have complete trust in your ability."

With Lincoln and Reece's decision, it was two votes to one. Kennedy had to go along with the majority decision. "It's not that I doubted your judgement Lincoln, I just want us to be sure we are making the right decision. This is our entrance into the millionaire's club, so we must protect our investment. Okay, so the decision is made, lets run with it," he agreed.

The boys sat round and had a few beers and talked about their love life. Kennedy wanted to know if Reece and Lily were lovers, as this had been tormenting him, and he had to know. He was surprised when Reece told him: not yet, as he respected her and would not take advantage of her until she was ready. This gave Kennedy some heart; she was still a virgin, and he was hoping she would belong to him before too long. He was still dating, but no one had come anywhere near Lily. He could still remember the warmth that had passed from her body to his during their hug on quiz night and the effect it had on him. Even just thinking about her set his heart racing. It was driving him mad. Apart from money, this was the one thing he wanted most, and his self-belief led him to believe that very soon, she would become his possession.

Tonight, the phone went in Kennedy's pad and it was Marcia. "Hello, Kennedy, I have been waiting on you to call me, so I decided to make the move. I have booked a table for the two of us to have dinner, say, Thursday night at Lugano's on High Street."

Kennedy did not have to wait to give his reply. "I'm sorry, Marcia, I go to the university quiz on Thursday nights, with Lincoln and Reece."

"Perhaps I could come along to the quiz and we could have a drink together?"

This, he did not want to happen, as Lily would be there, and he didn't need Marcia spoiling his night. "Perhaps another night, definitely not quiz night, thank you Marcia," and he hung up.

It was Thursday night and the team were all set for the quiz. Lily looked her lovely self, and Kennedy noticed she was taking more care in her dress. Was this because of Reece, or was it for his benefit? (Silly man; he had read it all wrong.)

Just as the papers were being handed out, there were wolf-whistles ringing out around the bar. Through the lounge-bar door came Marcia in a body-hugging pantsuit, her blonde hair was swished up in a bun. She looked so glamourous that all the blokes were ogling her. As soon as she saw Kennedy, she went over to their table.

Lily pounced. "Pull up a chair and join us, Marcia, we are just about to begin. You may be a good help to us."

Marcia thanked Lily, although she was surprised to see her here at the quiz with the boys.

Kennedy was furious: what the hell was Lily thinking of, inviting her to sit at their table?

"Right, we are about to begin. Quiet everyone," called the quiz master. The first five questions were called out and much discussion was had. Kennedy and Lily were at it again, both differing in the answers.

"For goodness' sake Lily, what do you know?" asked Marcia.

"I know I am right with this; it was part of my thesis. Believe me Kennedy."

With this he backed down and conceded. Several more questions came under review, but he was not going to be belittled in front of Marcia.

"Give him a break, Lily. You think you know it all," snapped Marcia.

This annoyed Reece, so he had his say. "More times than enough, Lily is right. She is the quiz champ here in this room, and she has helped us win many prizes, hasn't she Kennedy?" This he had to concede to, and he did not need Marcia fighting his battles. What the hell was she even doing here?

Reece took the papers up to be marked, and now it was drink time. Lily went up to the bar to buy Reece and herself a drink. As she stood at the bar Marcia came up beside her. "Leave Kennedy alone," she whispered.

"What do you mean?" asked Lily.

"I have noticed how he looks at you."

"You have it all wrong. I am in love with Reece. Kennedy is the last guy I would be interested in," she told Marcia, as she picked up her drinks and walked back to the table. With this Marcia signalled to Kennedy to come to the bar, as she didn't want him to be near Lily.

Next, the big announcement. "Once again, the top team have won. Would the young lady from team 'three plus one' come up and collect the money?" Lily walked up to collect their prize and as she walked past Marcia, she heard her say, "You should be collecting the prize, Kennedy. You knew most of the answers." Lily just ignored her but decided that from then on Kennedy could collect the prize money if it was that big a deal.

Now it was time for Marcia to let out some home truths while she had Kennedy to herself. "Did you know Lily said you would be the last person she would date?"

"How do you know that? It's not true." He was shocked by her statement.

"I told her to leave you alone and that's what she told me."

Kennedy was in total disbelief. In his own mind he thought this was a ploy by Marcia, so she could have him to herself. Lily would not have said that, he convinced himself.

"I can see you are hurt by Lily's words. You like her, but she loves Reece. You are not in the picture so forget her. I'm here for you Kennedy," she announced.

With this he picked up his beer and walked back to their table, leaving her standing. She wasn't alone for long, as there was a sudden swarm of bees around the honeypot. Kennedy sat quietly trying to absorb what Marcia had told him. Did Lily really think that of him?

Six months on

Today Lincoln rang the lads and arranged a meeting, as he had some important news for them. He had learnt of a ransomware attack that had affected between 800 and 1500 businesses and the company that was attacked was Kaseya. This meant all the companies that were using their software were affected. Intruders had gained control of its system, encrypting its data and demanding payment in cryptocurrency, in return for a key to decrypt the hostage data. Kaseya shut down its network as soon as it discovered the attack, so no more businesses were affected. He wondered how Kennedy would feel now if they had gone with this company.

Reece and Kennedy were in good fettle as they arrived at Lincoln's pad. They wondered what the meeting was about, as he had said it was important. When Lincoln reported to them what he knew, they looked at each other in stunned silence. A flood of relief came over Kennedy; thank goodness he was talked out of signing up with the company. If it had gone ahead, they would be having to find ransom money to retrieve their currency. The attackers would only accept cryptocurrency, so this would have meant part of their investment would be gone!

"Thank you, guys. I feel sick thinking about what may have happened. In future I will keep my mouth shut," admitted Kennedy. It was hard for him to admit he nearly made a big mistake.

"Do they know who was behind this attack?" asked Reece.

Lincoln explained they were the two big players in cyber-crime. They sell their software to criminal gangs, who have the contacts to move it on to unsuspecting investors. The two big players were heads of government in their countries, who could manipulate funds, and as long as they received part of the crypto loot, nothing else mattered.

Now for some good news. "Guess what lads? We have joined the ranks of billionaires. This calls for a celebration, so let's crack a bottle of bubbly," announced Lincoln. Silence had now turned to jubilation; they had made it to the top, and their dreams were realised.

As the third bottle was about to run out and the lads were drowning in their success, the conversation turned to their love lives. "Have you made love to Lily yet?" asked Kennedy. Reece sheepishly admitted they were now lovers and had even talked of moving in together. In fact, it was going to happen at the end of the month.

"We love each other. She is a beautiful girl, and I am going to ask her to marry me. I couldn't imagine anyone else in my life; she is my soulmate."

"Isn't that too soon? You haven't known each other for long," said Kennedy.

"My heart tells me she is the one, she is such fun to be with. We have intelligent conversations; she even topped her class this semester and to think her ambition is to be a high court judge. I couldn't be prouder," said a happy Reece.

Kennedy excused himself and went to the bathroom. He hoped the tears didn't come until he got there. His heart was broken. Lily was meant to belong to him; how was he going to survive without her? He had bedded many girls, but none had stirred up his feelings like when he felt Lily's body close to his that night of the quiz. He only needed to touch her and his blood ran wild. Many times when he was making love, if he didn't think it was Lily, his body let him down. He was a disappointment to himself and his lovers. Kennedy could not embarrass himself any longer, so he gave up on dating. He lived for his quiz nights when he could share a table with Lily. All the money in the world had not made him completely happy, and he was a lonely billionaire with no one.

Three years had passed and today it was Lily's graduation. She was now a qualified lawyer with an honours degree. Reece had asked Lincoln and Kennedy to bring their respective partners so they could celebrate together.

Lincoln arrived with Sophie, but Kennedy came alone. The boys worried about him as he was not his bright confident self, and hadn't been for a long while, but he wouldn't tell them what was bothering him. He wasn't dating; instead he was brooding.

Kennedy watched as Lily was capped, and he felt so proud of her. His body ached as he thought about her. She was an intelligent, happy young lady, but alas she was not his. He knew today he could get close to her as he congratulated her on her success. Their bodies would meet, he could not wait. Was that special feeling of excitement still there? It wouldn't be long before he found out.

As Lily came towards their group Reece was the first to congratulate and hug her. "I'm so proud of you Lily, I love you to bits," he affectionately told her. Lincoln and Sophie both hugged her and offered their congratulations. Now the time had come for Kennedy to have his turn. He took her in his arms and the moment his body touched hers, a rush of blood flooded through him, he felt weak, he wanted her at that moment, but then reality set in and he realised he was never going to have her.

The group headed off to the university pub on the corner of High Street where all the students drank. It was so crowded today and everyone was packed in like sardines, with hardly standing room. It was at this moment Kennedy seized his opportunity. He sidled up to Lily and put his hand on her waist then let it slide down to her thigh. She felt warm and inviting. People were being pushed against each other, and he agonised whether he should go a step further; his body was edging him on. This was the closest he had got to touching her, when suddenly she was shoved backwards and he had to grab her to stop her falling. While doing so, his hand brushed her breasts as he steadied her. He was consumed with love, and prayed he could hold her forever, but this was not to be, as Lily was apologising to him and thanking him for saving her.

Reece came to the rescue and suggested they go back to his pad and continue celebrating there. He wanted to make an announcement and tell everyone that they had bought a nice home and would be moving in at the end of the month, as they were thinking ahead, family wise. Lily had been offered a position with a prominent law firm. Of course, with this announcement came sadness. The very mention of children to Kennedy's ears spelt the end.

Several weeks later when the lads were at Lincoln's pad the financial news was not great. The bitcoin had dropped in value, and they were no longer billionaires. They had been reduced to millionaires. To the average person this seemed trivial, but in the investment sector it was not good news. All they could do was wait to see if the currency corrected itself. It was here he told Lincoln and Kennedy he would not be at the quiz night as he was flying to a conference for seven days, but Lily would still come along. Kennedy offered to pick her up and see her home after the quiz finished. Reece took him up on this offer as he knew she would be in safe hands.

As Reece was driving back to his pad he wondered if he should tell Lily he was adopted. Each time he went to tell her, he changed his mind and wondered if he had not come to terms with it himself. No one else knew; he had not told anyone, not even Lincoln or Kennedy. One day the time would be right, but that wasn't now.

Lily said goodbye to Reece as she dropped him off at the airport. She would miss him, but he had to go to this conference. She assured him she would be fine, as when he came home, they would be shifting into their new home, so she had plenty of packing to keep her occupied at nights. She would be at work during the day. She loved her new work environment, the people were friendly and she had been given clients to look after, so was establishing herself as a lawyer. Reece had told her Kennedy would take her to the quiz night and she was happy about that, not that she felt a closeness to him. There was something about him, but because he was Reece's friend, she tolerated him. Reece had told her that it was his parents' money that got them started into cryptocurrency, and they needed each other, as each had a different field of expertise. That was why they were a formidable team, and their reliance on each other was crucial for them to succeed in the crypto world. Lincoln and his partner had become good friends with them, but Kennedy remained a mystery.

Tonight was quiz night so Lily waited for Kennedy to arrive. She was dressed in a cotton frock as it was a hot night and once in the bar sometimes it was stifling, depending on the crowd. She heard the car horn toot, so locked the door and walked down the path. As soon as Kennedy saw her walking towards him, his heartbeat rose and for a moment, he pretended she was his love that he was meeting. He didn't get out and open the car door but let Lily do that, which was just a true reflection of himself. As she climbed in, he remarked how nice she looked tonight.

"But I always look nice, don't I?" she asked.

Was she flirting he wondered; he thought so. "Yes, Lily, you are a beautiful intelligent lady."

They drove the rest of the way in silence. When they arrived at the pub, Kennedy got out of the car and walked around to open the door. Tonight, they would have to find a fourth person to form their team. Lincoln had a table ready for them, so after their greetings they sat down. New people who wanted to join a quiz team stood by the bar at a certain place, so teams looking for another person knew where to find them. Lincoln spotted a young lady who he thought might cheer Kennedy up, so he invited her to come and join them. She introduced herself as Katelin, a third-year student studying anthropology. The two girls talked away while the boys collected the quiz papers.

"Quiet everyone," said the quizmaster. Now it was all go. Once again Lily and Kennedy differed on several answers, but tonight his bolshiness seemed to have disappeared. Katelin answered a couple of questions, so Lincoln hoped there might be a connection between her and Kennedy. If so, he would drive Lily home. Come the end of the night, there was a tie for first place, their team and another, so the prize money was shared. Lincoln asked Kennedy to go to the bar with him, so he could suss out whether he wanted to take Katelin home. The answer came back as no. He was taking Lily home, so it was left at that.

As they pulled up at Reece's pad, Kennedy got out and opened the door for Lily. As she climbed out, she thanked him, but he insisted on seeing her to the door. When they stood there, he asked Lily if she would make him a cup of coffee. Out of the goodness of her heart she invited him in and put the kettle on. When she brought the coffee to the table, he was staring at her and his gaze never left her. She felt a bit uneasy so asked him if he was alright.

"No, I am not Lily. I don't know if you have noticed, but I'm in love with you."

This took her by complete surprise. "Don't be silly, Kennedy. I love Reece; we are engaged," she told him.

"I want you, Lily, I don't go out with girls any more. I'm waiting for you to belong to me."

This put Lily in panic mode. "Please go, this is not right, go now."

"No, Lily, I'm not leaving. If I can't have you, I am going to take you now," he said as he got up from his chair. He walked over and picked her up and carried her to the bedroom. Lily put up a struggle, but her small frame was no match for Kennedy's strapping body. She was petrified; what was going to happen next? He pushed her down on the bed and ripped her dress off, as she tried to break free. He dropped his trousers and climbed on top of her. "I've waited for three years to have you, Lily. Now I don't have to wait any longer. Tonight you will belong to me."

His hands slid down her body and he pulled down her knickers. Just feeling her so close to him was the most wonderful feeling, and he knew his body would respond tonight; he would not have to feel embarrassed or humiliated. Lily was so frightened, she just lay there and let him do what he wanted, then it would all be over. He kissed her body and fondled her breasts, then let his hands wander down her thighs. It was then he started to cry. "I love you, Lily. I won't hurt you I promise. We must become one. I must have something to remember you by. Please don't hate me. I can never love anyone else."

Lily had never seen a grown man cry, and her heart felt sad. Kennedy needed to be pitied, but what he was doing was wrong. She closed her eyes and tried to blank out what was happening from her mind. If she tried to fight him off, would he get angry, then turn violent? She wished he would finish his business, then he hopefully would leave, so she could have a long hot shower. But Kennedy had other ideas, as he wanted to spend the night lying next to her, just to be able to touch her when he needed to.

If it had been anyone else other than Kennedy, Lily would have fought like hell, but she knew he hadn't been himself lately, so didn't know what sort of mood he was in, and whether he would become violent. She lay still as he rolled off her and cuddled into her back. She could hear him whimpering, apologising for what he had done, but at the same time proclaiming his love for her. She had no idea this is how he felt about her, as there didn't seem to be any signs that she had noticed.

"Please don't tell Reece. He must never know; he is my best friend," he begged. "Promise me, Lily, I'm sorry but I had to have you. You will never know how much you mean to me. I will remember this night forever." Within minutes he was sound asleep. Lily lay there for a little while, then she left the bed and went to shower. She had to rid Kennedy from her body. She knew he was remorseful and all she could feel was pity for him. She wasn't frightened any more; he was a lost soul in need of help. He would have to live with this for the rest of his life and each time he saw Reece, he would be reminded of his sin.

When she went back to the bedroom Kennedy was gone. She looked out the window and his car was no longer parked in the driveway. She ripped the sheets off the bed and bundled them up, ready to take them to the rubbish bin, as she wanted no reminders of Kennedy in the flat. But then she noticed her dress and knickers were missing…

Lily watched as the plane landed; she couldn't wait to see Reece again. Was she going to be able to put what happened behind her? She made a promise to herself she would never tell Reece, as she didn't want to ruin their relationship. They had been friends long before she came on the scene. She felt safe with Reece's arms around her; it was as if he was her protector.

He was full of talk about the conference and the people he had meet, which she was happy about, as it hid her silence. This was going to be the biggest hurdle, the guilt. Would it disappear? She had to keep telling herself it was not her fault.

"Did you miss me?" he asked. Lily held on to him and assured him it was good to have him home with her.

"Have you seen the lads?" he asked. Lily told him she had seen them at the quiz.

"Did Kennedy pick you up and drop you home as he promised?" Lily answered with a quick yes, then changed the subject.

That night when they went to bed, Reece wanted to make love to Lily, and she had to fight her demons and pretend all was well, when it was not. She wondered how long she would have to put up with this feeling of guilt. She was thankful Reece hadn't noticed her indifference. It was not until the morning she realised she hadn't taken her precaution, but didn't worry too much as one night, surely, she wouldn't get pregnant. Then her mind went back to when Kennedy had taken her: had she used precaution that night?

Come quiz night, Lily tried to get out of going, but Reece insisted she went. She knew she would have to face Kennedy at some stage, and the longer she put it off, the worse it would become. She plucked up courage and when they arrived only Lincoln was there.

"Where's Kennedy?" asked Reece.

"He rang me and said he wouldn't be here. I'm worried about him Reece; he only leaves his pad to go to work. He doesn't date any more. What has happened to our party boy? He never misses the quiz," said Lincoln.

"There's Katelin, I'll asked her to join us again tonight," and with this Lily called out to her, and over she came to join them. Lily felt sad for Kennedy, as only she knew what was wrong.

Reece said he would go and see Kennedy the next night and see what was bothering him. They missed him at the quiz as there was no banter between him and Lily. Tonight, they only managed second place. "He's got to come back, we need him," said Lincoln. Lily wondered if she should visit him and let him know he was forgiven, that she wanted life to continue as it was before that fateful night. But she would wait until Reece had been to see him.

After Reece's visit, he told Lily that Kennedy had hugged him and said he was sorry. "I can't understand what he has to be sorry about; he has done nothing wrong. There is something troubling him. I'm worried. Do you think you could talk to him?" he asked Lily. She said she would see him tomorrow.

As Lily pulled up Kennedy's driveway, she didn't know how she would feel when she came face to face with him, but there was only one way to find out! She rang the doorbell and when he came to the door, she got the shock of her life. He looked as if he had never slept for days, his face was puffed up and his eyes red.

"Kennedy, you look terrible. What is wrong?" she asked.

He stood silent, then the tears started, "I'm sorry, please forgive me, Lily," he sobbed.

She moved close to him and hugged him. "You are forgiven, Kennedy. You were gentle with me, but you know it was wrong. Let us get on with our lives. Find someone else and move forward."

"I made a promise to you, Lily, I will never love anyone else. I have never known such love, but I know you will never be mine. I have a reminder of you, each night when I go to bed, that is all I need."

"What do you mean, Kennedy?" she asked. He told her he had her dress and underwear and it stayed under his pillow.

Tears rolled down Lily's face. How sad that it had come to this. "I want you to promise me you will come to quiz nights. We all love you, Kennedy, so for my sake do this for me."

They held on to each other and she heard him whisper, "For you I will do anything."

On this note Lily kissed him on his cheek and said, "See you on Thursday night. Promise?"

It was quiz night again. Lily felt sure Kennedy would be there as she had made him promise. When she and Reece arrived, Lincoln was there on his own, and she felt let down, but it wasn't long before Kennedy turned up. He greeted them and seemed to be back to his old self. They had the dream team back, so it was down to business, and tonight they were going to regain their position as the top team.

Kennedy and Lily were up to their old tricks, so, yes, it

was back to normal. She kept her eyes away from him, for fear he might slip back into a depressed state. When the quiz finished, he took the papers up to be marked, while Reece brought back drinks for them. They sat and talked about Reece's time away, which was when Kennedy left the table and went to the bathroom. Lily waited for him to come back to the table, as she knew he felt guilty, the signs were there when he returned, his eyes were red. She knew he had shed tears, in silence. Then the winners of the quiz were announced, 'Three plus one'. Lily told Kennedy to go and collect the prize money.

Several months went by with no incidents, apart from Lily feeling sick in the mornings. She thought it was just the flu so battled on at work. This went on for a couple of weeks, then all was back to normal. It wasn't until she found difficulty fitting into her clothes that she decided it was time to go to the doctor. When the tests were carried out, it was found she was pregnant. Lily was in shock as it was only one night when she forgot her protection: the night Reece came home from his conference. Then she had a reality check. What about the night Kennedy slept with her? There were only six days between the two incidents. 'Oh my God,' she whispered to herself, this was just too much to take in, her brain shut down, she couldn't cope with what she was confronted with! She worried what Reece would think, as they had not discussed starting a family. She decided not to tell him now, as guilt came to back to haunt her.

Before long Reece noticed Lily was putting on weight, so mentioned this to her. Now was the time to come clean, Lily thought. "Reece, I am pregnant; I couldn't tell you as we had never discussed starting a family." There was silence for a minute.

"I am so happy, Lily. You should have told me. How long have you known?"

When she told him she was nearly five months' pregnant, she started to cry. He was so calm about all this and so accepting, but she felt overwhelmed.

That night there was a meeting at Lincoln's pad, as it was time for them to check their cryptocurrency to see how much was in their wallet. They had made a rule only to check every three months, otherwise they would always be looking. All their bitcoin transactions are recorded on a public ledger, known as the blockchain. Reece and Kennedy didn't quite understand all the working of this system, so they relied heavily on Lincoln. He was the key figure for their crypto investments. Tension was building as he pulled up their wallet.

"Guess what lads, we are on the way up again." A collective sigh of relief was heard, as Lincoln spelt out the welcome news.

"There is much talk in the financial sector about a new phenomenon called NFTs. They are digital collectable projects. Have you heard about them Lincoln?" asked Kennedy. Lincoln acknowledged that he had, but he would have to study them more closely, before he could give an informed opinion.

"How do they differ to cryptocurrency?" asked Reece.

Kennedy went on to explain that cryptocurrency was a fungible asset and used for financial transactions and are interchangeable; a bitcoin for a bitcoin, whereas NFTs are non-fungible, something that people can buy, sell and speculate with, such as real estate, art, cars, sports memorabilia, in other words collectables.

"Give me time and I will work out if I think we should look into it," Lincoln said. The lads were happy to be guided by him, as he could use his knowledge to suss out what was a safe investment.

As the meeting ended, Reece broke the news that Lily was pregnant. It was a surprise, but they were both thrilled. "When did you find out?" asked Kennedy. Reece explained they had worked it out to be when he came back from the conference. Lincoln expressed his congratulations, followed by a hesitant Kennedy.

"Well, guys," said Reece, "I had never thought of becoming a father so soon, as I was too wrapped up in our cryptocurrency, but now I have another interest."

Over the following months Lily's body gradually expanded, and she glowed in pregnancy. She was happy and very much in love with Reece. They spent hours sorting out baby names. If it was a little girl, Reece wanted to call her Leila, a name close to her mother's. Lily decided on Bradley for a boy's name, and this is where it stood momentarily, but things could change. Lily had stopped going to the quiz nights as she found it too uncomfortable, and she was sorely missed, as they didn't take out the top spot as often. Each week Lincoln and Reece tried to choose a team member that would take Kennedy's eye, but sadly he showed no interest. They were perplexed; what was wrong with him? He was the playboy, but he didn't even talk about the opposite sex, which was so out of character for him. In the past he was the one who boasted about his conquests. There had been several talks with Kennedy, as they were a little worried about him, but he seemed happy enough, so they just left it at that. Perhaps one day he might say something.

Today Kennedy was visiting Reece and Lily when she felt the baby moving. Reece told Kennedy to put his hand on Lily's belly so he could feel it. As he rested his hand on her, he felt a little kick, and suddenly that longing feeling was back, that wonderful warmth that passed from her to him was there once again. He wanted his hand to rest there forever, he felt as if she was his, as his love had never waned. It didn't seem to matter if it was her touch, her speech or just being in her company, he felt happy, and no one else mattered to him.

That night as Kennedy lay in bed cuddled up to Lily's dress, he thought of her little baby. He envied Reece, and he would never have a family of his own. Apart from Lily he couldn't make anyone else happy, his body would not perform, and he was left embarrassed and confused. He then thought back to when Reece said she had fallen pregnant, when he came back from the conference. It was then he realised it was only five days before that he had made love to her. Could there be a possibility that he might be the father? Was the baby his and Lily's? With this thought in mind, he cried into Lily's dress. Maybe he could be a father after all. He would hold on to this faint hope, but how would he ever know.

It was Friday night and the lads were meeting at Lincoln's pad to discuss the new cool trend, NFTs. Lincoln had to explain to Reece what these were. He said this stood for 'non-fungible tokens'.

"What does non-fungible mean?" asked Reece.

"It means that it is completely unique. Token means it can be transferred on a blockchain. They are assets that carry their own unique digital identity," explained Lincoln.

"What can you do with them?" Reece wanted to know.

Lincoln went on to explain they were collectables such as art, coins, cars, property and sports memorabilia, anything that is easy interchangeable. For example, it is one thing to hold one of millions of reproductions of an artwork, but to hold a piece that can be directly traced to its creator is the ultimate. These are items that cannot be evenly divided and interchanged for the same value. For example, diamonds are unique and cannot be duplicated or swapped.

After listening intently to Lincoln's explanations, Reece wondered if perhaps they should delve into NFTs. "Would you be willing to give it a go?" he asked.

Lincoln replied, "Let us think about it for another week, as I need to know that it is a safe investment. I have been told people buy them for an attached value of importance, rather than the need to own the actual asset. We don't need to prove ourselves; we have made it to the top, so let us be sure and understand the true value of NFTs. I will probe the internet and see what people are saying about them. I will find out if they are 'for or against', and this way we can make a decision."

The meeting ended and the lads bid each other goodnight.

The new arrival

Reece and Lily were now parents to a baby girl. Lily had been in labour for twenty-four hours, so was exhausted when baby Leila arrived. She was drifting off to sleep as Reece was rubbing her forehead. Leila had been taken away so Lily could get some much-needed sleep. She had asked Reece to be with her for the birth, so now he knew what women went through and he was astounded at the amount of pain involved. This sealed his love for Lily.

He couldn't wait to tell his friends that he now had his little girl and all went well. The nurse came in and told him to go home, as Lily would probably sleep for a good six hours. He asked to see Leila before he left, as he wanted to take her image with him. There she lay sound asleep, such a little button all wrapped up, without a worry in the world. She was beautiful; he felt so proud!

He decided to visit Kennedy as he was near his pad; he

had to share his joy with someone. He knocked on his door and when Kennedy opened it, Reece hugged him and told him he was a father to baby Leila. "Oh, so you have a little girl, that is wonderful. Come and let us wet her head," he said. He walked over to his drink cabinet and opened a bottle of red wine, so they sat down, and he wanted to know all about Lily and the baby. Reece told him about the birth, and this was the news Kennedy wanted to hear. He had to know; this was his Lily he was hearing about, and perhaps his baby.

"What does Leila look like?' he wanted to know.

Reece said she was beautiful, so tiny, just a little button.

"Does she look like Lily?" he asked.

Poor Reece, he had forgotten already, but then he had only seen her for a few seconds. The lads had many cheers, both with their own thoughts, each thinking they were the father!

The next morning when Reece woke up his head was not at all clear. He had to have a shower and get to the hospital to see Lily and his new daughter. The celebrations had gone on into the small hours of the morning so he hadn't had much sleep. He was surprised that Kennedy was so interested in the baby. He had never seen him so excited for a long time. Was this because he didn't have a girlfriend? Was the baby a distraction from dating? Reece still worried why Kennedy had lost interest in the opposite sex. It was so out of character for him. Perhaps he should again have a private word with him.

Several nights after giving birth Lily woke to find the

most beautiful vase of flowers sitting on her hospital dresser. There was a note accompanying them: 'I'm so proud of you, love Kennedy'. Her heart sank. Why did he do this? Did he still think the baby was his? Could she say it was not? No, she simply didn't know. But in her own mind it was her and Reece's baby, that's all she wanted to believe. Lily still had memories of the night Kennedy raped her; surely a baby could not have been conceived from an act carried out against her will? Perhaps she was reading the wrong message into this. Was he just being a good friend? When Reece came to visit and saw the flowers, he knew who they were from, as Kennedy had told him Lily deserved them as this was the first baby born into their tightknit friendship. A special occasion for all!

Lily had only been home for two days when she received a visit from Kennedy. Reece had been called back to work and she was home alone. She felt a little awkward as she answered the door with Leila in her arms. She invited him in and he asked if he could hold the baby, so she gave her to him. Kennedy told Lily that Leila was beautiful and the name suited her. He talked away to Leila, which totally surprised Lily, as she didn't think he was the nurturing kind. Little did she know, holding his baby sent a rush of adrenaline through his body. He so wanted to say something to Lily, but he knew it would cause an upset and he did not want this, as he hoped to visit often and cuddle his little girl.

Lily was actually starting to warm to him, as his bolshiness had disappeared, and she saw a softer side to him, something she had not noticed before. If for one moment she knew what he was thinking, however, her thoughts would change.

One year had passed and it was Leila's first birthday. Tonight, there was a birthday celebration, and the lads and their partners were invited. Lincoln arrived with his partner who was now his fiancée, and Kennedy arrived on his own. Leila had just found her walking legs and was holding on to things as she toddled from one object to the next. She was putting on a display for her guests who were intrigued. She was a happy soul, but there was one person she always made for – that was Kennedy. He was her favourite as he spoilt her. No one seemed to worry about this, because he didn't have anyone. He always gravitated towards Leila. When Reece and Lily wanted a night out, they called on Kennedy to babysit, as there was a special bond forming between him and Leila. As soon as she saw him, she always expected him to lift her up and cuddle her. While she was in his arms, he would tell her she was as beautiful as her mother.

As the night progressed and all the birthday duties were over, the drink flowed and everyone was starting to talk freely. As he consumed more alcohol, Kennedy's love for his two girls was hard to conceal. Lily noticed this, so she asked him to come into the kitchen, as she wanted to talk to him.

"I think it would be better if you leave, Kennedy. I will call you a taxi," she told him.

"No, Lily, I want to stay with my two girls."

"Please, Kennedy, I beg you to go now. Don't embarrass anyone," she pleaded.

"But, Lily, Leila could be our daughter, you know that. I love you both, and there will never be anyone else in my life. I won't cause a scene, so ring me a taxi and I will go. I just had to say this to you."

She was taken by surprise; did he really think Leila could be his? As she gave this some thought, doubt started to creep in, and she could not be sure either way. When the taxi arrived, she couldn't get him out the door quick enough. He didn't protest, but he left her with, "I love our little girl, Lily. She is what I live for."

As the weeks went by, Lily was still working from home. Her life was busy and her clientele was growing. The company needed her back at work in the office, as clients wanted to have face-to-face contact with her. Lily suggested they hire a nanny to care for Leila in their own home, so this was decided on. Lily felt guilty as she loved being a hands-on mother, but she was still aspiring to become a high court judge. Today she had a client who wanted to find out if he was the biological father of his ex-partner's daughter. This stirred her own thoughts; she had been wondering about this lately, as Kennedy spent a lot of time with Leila. She agreed to take on the case, and perhaps she could unravel her own dilemma alongside her client's. In the meantime, Reece wanted a playmate for Leila, so they decided not to use contraceptives and let nature take its course. It was better to have their family now, then she could carry on with her career without any interruptions in the future.

First, Lily had to get her client to bring in a sample of his hair, along with that of his ex-partner and the daughter. He didn't know how long it would take to get these samples, so Lily told him she couldn't proceed until he brought them to her. She spent the next week studying up on DNA. A child's DNA contains code that represents characteristics of both parents. Every child has 46 chromosomes, 23 from the mother and 23 from the father. Comparing the DNA sequence of a child to that of an alleged father can show if the child's DNA was derived from that man or not. This was frightening for Lily; what if Leila was Kennedy's baby, did she really want to know, and if this was so, how would she cope with this discovery?

She managed to get a sample of Kennedy's hair along with Reece's, so put them in their separate envelopes. Now she had to pluck a hair from Leila. She felt nervous as she handed them to the laboratory assistant. He said to give him a week, then come back and he hopefully would have the results.

The next week felt like a lifetime. She wanted to know, then the next minute she changed her mind, then came back to the first thought – her mind was all over the place. The day before she was due to go to find the results, the laboratory assistant called and asked her to come in, as he had some questions to ask her. What could he want to know? Lily had a client to see, so as soon as she finished, she picked up her files and drove to the laboratory. The assistant asked her to sit down, then he started, "Tell me, Lily, the two persons' DNA you brought in, are they related?"

Lily looked startled, "No, they are just friends, they met at university, why did you ask that?"

The assistant replied, "That's strange, because both DNAs are a close match. No one's is identical, but they are carrying a similar amount of chromosomal data. Are you sure they aren't close relations?"

Lily couldn't believe what she was hearing. How could Kennedy and Reece be related? Their lives were so different.

"Could there be any other explanation?" she asked.

"No, because their chromosomal data was such a close match, it points to one conclusion, they could have shared the same mother but a different father. Perhaps you could trace their backgrounds through the birth, deaths and marriages, and this may prove they are indeed related. Now do you want to know who the baby's father is?"

Lily had had enough shock for one day, she certainly couldn't take any more. "No, please could you keep this information and when I am ready, I will come back and talk to you." With this Lily thanked the assistant and hurriedly left the laboratory. She was so overcome with what she had been told. Reece and Kennedy, how on earth could they be related? They hadn't known each other until they met at varsity. Her head was swirling. She could not talk to Reece about this; it was something she had to solve on her own. Where to from here?

Lily could not let this sit dormant, she had to find out

as it was driving her mad. She questioned Reece about his parents: did they have any other children that they might have adopted out?

"Why are you asking all these questions, Lily?" he wanted to know. Did she know about his adoption, should he tell her? Perhaps now was the right time.

"I have not told you this, as I am still coming to terms with it myself, but I only found out after my parents died that I was adopted. It wasn't until my aunty told me, and by then it was too late to ask any questions. I still feel they were my true mother and father as I loved them dearly."

This confession hit Lily like a lightning bolt, and she felt numb. Was the puzzle beginning to fall into place, could what she was told in fact be true? She cuddled Reece and said she was sorry for him, to learn about his adoption from his aunty.

"Yes, it hurt at the time, but I don't think about it now. Look how well off they left me. To me they were my true parents."

"Do you ever want to find your biological mother?" Lily asked.

"No, I have no desire to go there. My life is what I remember and that is the way I want it to stay," he told Lily.

Now she knew that if she was to go ahead with solving the close DNA, she would be on her own.

As she lay in bed that night, all these wild thoughts were flooding her brain. What would happen if Reece and Kennedy were indeed related? What avenue would she pursue? Perhaps she would talk to Kennedy about his background, then do some digging. He was only too happy to talk with Lily about anything, just being near her was where he wanted to be. The opportunity arose two days later when he came around to see Leila. Reece was at work on a late afternoon shift, so she had Kennedy to herself.

"Kennedy, you haven't talked much about your family. Tell me about them. In all the time we have known each other, I know very little about your life."

"There's not much to tell. My parents were childhood sweethearts, but they split several times. They had a rocky relationship until my mother left, leaving Dad to look after my sister and me. We never heard from her after she walked out. Dad did his best and put us both through university. He sacrificed a lot for us, so I made a promise to myself to care for him, as that's the least he deserves. Other than that, there's not much else exciting to report. I do not know if my mother still has our surname, 'Barkley', but perhaps one day she might want to make contact with us."

Lily took this all in, then asked what his mother's first name was. "Dad called her Lauren; I think she was Lauren Rainer before she met him. Apparently, they were lovers while at school then they broke up and got together again. This was the pattern, an on-again, off-again relationship. Dad never worried about another partner."

"Oh, that's sad," sympathised Lily. Now she had more than enough leads to proceed to the next stage, a visit to the registrar of birth, deaths and marriages.

It was Friday night and the lads were at Lincoln's pad

as it was time to see how their investment was doing. There had been whispers that the cryptocurrency had taken a tumble, which was their biggest fear, but they knew of its volatility and its speculative nature. In the investment world, one must prepare for ups and downs. They gathered around Lincoln's computer and waited until he opened their wallet. To their dismay their fortunes had all but halved, but they were still in the millionaire bracket. Only because of the amount of money Reece had inherited were they able to buy a large amount of bitcoin at the measly price of $150 per coin. It then shot up to $62,000 per coin, but now it had slid down to $42,000.

This is not what they wanted to see, they had gone from billionaires to mere millionaires, and this was not easily accepted by these eager young men. Lincoln was the stable influence, telling them it would rise again, as that was the nature of the beast. It was what he called a floating fortune! It was still known as the currency of the future, especially in the younger generation. It was recorded that cryptocurrency had topped 1.5 trillion globally. Kennedy studied the markets and bitcoin was the most liquid digital asset on the market because of technology. Supply and demand are one of the leading factors that causes the rise and fall of cryptocurrencies, so this they would keep their eyes on.

Kennedy was well up in the financial sector, so he had developed a sense of what was a good investment. NFTs were now being talked about and people were starting to investigate their place in the up-and-coming market. The talk was that there was a renewed interest, in fact a boom, in digital art, and this had thrust NFTs into mainstream consciousness. Digital art gives power back to the creators and the buyers, who entrust in the decentralised system to come up with a fair price. The buzz and the interest make the price … it's that simple. It left the people to decide, not the third parties and the meddlers, who are known to set standards or fix prices. This is what the crypto world is all about, cutting out the third persons, governments and banks, letting money and people move more freely without restrictions.

Kennedy liked the idea that it was up to people to make their own decisions, not be ruled by bureaucracy … it would change the internet, even real life. This was giving power back to the people; this is what the young guns were seeking and why the world of cryptocurrency was right up there. But often with these get-rich-quick schemes came 'boom and bust' due to their volatility, as there were no rules in place, and it was up to the investors themselves to set the scene.

Kennedy took time to reminisce on what his father told him about his younger days. First there was the barter system, then to the precious metals, to paper notes and now to a system where people's wealth was hidden in a wallet on a computer. How the world had changed. Now that the young guns were computer savvy, it just took one clever person with a smart idea in the technology world and the excitement it brought with it. The clever tech-savvy young ones had a greater knowledge of maths and computer science associated with making and breaking codes. This has created some of the wildest and most volatile assets in existence. All these new terms such as ledgers, blockchain, decentralization and cryptography, which only this generation understands, all play a significant part in the cryptocurrency world.

Kennedy's father was getting older and had given up on his son's explanations and enthusiasm on how exciting the crypto world was. It was all beyond him! He was a little afraid of Kennedy's investments that lacked government control and protection. Who was in control? He brought this up with his son, only to be told, "Dad it's okay, don't worry, there is such a technology called blockchain and as many as one million computers can be connected, allowing transactions to be recorded and managed in a secure way, which makes it appealing." Even after this explanation, it was still beyond his father's comprehension.

"What has happened to the world? It has gone mad," he told his son.

Kennedy had kept the promise he made to himself to look after his father, so he could have a happy retirement, as it was his dad who put him through university and gave him a good education. There had still been no contact with his mother, which hurt deep down, especially now that he had a little girl, in his own thinking. He often thought he would like to tell his father that he had a granddaughter, but with this came shame, which he had to bear himself.

"Why haven't you got a girlfriend, Kennedy?" he asked his son. "I hope this crypto thing hasn't interfered with your personal life. It is time you settled down and started a family."

Kennedy hesitated before answering. "I am in love with someone, but she belongs to another. I can't forget her, so my social life is on hold."

His father was sad to hear this, as he thought his son would be a good catch. He was a decent young man with a sound brain. He decided to let it be at the moment, as he could see the hurt in his son's eyes.

The seeking begins

While looking at the microfiches in the genealogy section at the local library, Lily came across a female named Lauren Rainer who had registered a birth at the age of sixteen. There was no father's name on the microfiche, just her name and age. She then decided to go to the microfiches on marriages to see if and when there was a marriage date. This had taken up her lunch hour and she was due back in her office in five minutes, so had to settle for what she had discovered in this short time. It was a start, a good start, as now she knew that perhaps the baby was put up for adoption. Her mind came back to Reece: was he that baby? Surely not – it was impossible. Then her mind went back to what the laboratory assistant had said: that their DNAs were a close match. It all seemed too bizarre, and was she in fact starting to imagine all this?

That night while at home their peace was disturbed,

so Lily went to the door. It was Kennedy, who wanted to see Leila. Was she still up? It was about her bedtime. As soon as she heard Kennedy's voice, Leila let out a squeal and made her way around the furniture until she could reach his leg. He lifted her up and the banter began between them. Leila hugged and kissed him, knowing he loved this. Lily went to take her off him as it was her bedtime and it was then he said, "You are Daddy's little girl."

Lily looked to see if Reece was within hearing range, which he was. "Yes, she certainly is my little girl," he answered. Lily heaved a sigh of relief; thank God he didn't understand what Kennedy meant. She fired him a look of disapproval, at which he just smiled. The two boys went into the study, while Lily settled Leila down for the night. She was still shaking over what Kennedy had said.

Today Lily was back at the library searching the microfiches on marriages. She had to try and work back dates, otherwise she would be there for days on end. She worked out by Reece's age, roughly around those dates, given a year or two, when there may have been a marriage. Just as she was about to give up, there it was, 'marriage between Lauren Rainer and Joseph Barkley' on 14 March 1996.

Lily had no idea of Kennedy's age, and she had just presumed he was the same age as Reece, but this was turning out to not be the case. If he was born after their marriage and Reece was born before, then Reece was several years older. It was all one huge jigsaw puzzle, so was she finally making progress? The DNA test was right, there was a close connection between Reece and Kennedy; in fact they were half-brothers with the same mother.

Lily was shaken; where did this leave her? Leila's father was either one of the half-brothers, if she was Reece's, then Kennedy would be an uncle, and if she was Kennedy's then Reece would be an uncle. Oh my God, what a mess. Lily had to get out of the building and get some fresh air. Thank goodness she was the only one who harboured this information, but how long would it be before it reared its ugly head? Would this destroy the friendship between the lads? Then she remembered Reece's words when she asked him if he ever wanted to find out about his birth mother: "No, I have no desire to go there." Lily felt intense pressure building inside. She had discovered all this behind Reece's back, so how could she tell him … she simply could not.

Reece and Lily were still trying for another family member, but nothing was happening. They wondered why she fell pregnant so quick with Leila and now there was no sign of anything happening. Reece happened to mention this to Kennedy one day. It was the worst thing he could have done, as this made Kennedy believe even more that Leila was his daughter. He secretly hoped this was the proof he needed. If they never had any more babies, he was definitely the father. Reece had even talked about going to find out if the lack of conception was his fault, but Lily told him to wait and be patient, as it had happened once, so it would happen again. She prayed on her life that she became pregnant, and if not, then the unthinkable may turn out to be true.

· · ·

As the months went by, Lily worried about Reece's expectations for her to become pregnant as it had started to interfere with their love life. "If nothing happens within the next couple of months, I am going to see if there is something wrong with me," he told Lily. This sent her into a panic, as she had concluded that Leila must be Kennedy's baby, and that perhaps Reece couldn't father a child. If this was so, how was she going to explain Leila's conception? There seemed to be only one answer!

Tonight, Lily put on a low-cut dress and told Reece she was going out with friends from work, not to wait up as she would be home late. She drove around to Kennedy's pad and parked up. As she knocked on his door, he was surprised to find Lily standing there. "I thought I deserved a night out, so I've come to keep you company." Kennedy couldn't believe his eyes, as here was his Lily looking so lovely. "Would you like a wine?" he asked. Lily told him that would be nice, so he opened a bottle of red. They sat and talked, and Lily was enjoying his company, as Reece had been a bit on edge lately. She felt relaxed, secretly hoping Kennedy might carry her into his bedroom and take her. But as the night went by, he made no move towards her.

"I am so sorry for what I did to you, Lily. I love you, but that was no excuse. I live with my guilt every day. My feelings have never changed and never will, but I am living in hope that we both made a beautiful little girl."

Lily was touched by Kennedy's words. "I have forgiven

you, and yes perhaps we did make Leila, that's why I am here. Reece is thinking about getting checked to see why I haven't fallen pregnant, but I am frightened that he may not be able to father children, and if that is so, how do I explain Leila? Kennedy, I am sick with worry. I came tonight expecting to be raped."

"I would never do that to you again, Lily. You deserve better. I was an idiot, and I took away your dignity and your pride. I hurt you, and for that I have suffered."

Lily rested her hand on his lap, "This time I want you Kennedy. You were gentle with me and for that I forgave you. Please take me to bed. Let us make love." Kennedy was stunned; this situation he had dreamed of many times over, but now that he was confronted with it, it didn't seem right.

"Are you sure, my love? I was disrespectful to you and now you are asking me to bed you?"

"I want to have another baby, Kennedy, and this seems to be the only way it can happen. Please don't ask any more questions." Then the sobbing started. Kennedy stood up and took Lily in his arms and held her tight. He could smell her perfume, as her body came in contact with his; he felt tingles running up his spine. Excitement was building in his lower body, so he lifted her up and carried her through to his bed. Lily started to undress but Kennedy wanted to do this; here was the love of his life and he wanted to savour every moment. As he removed her clothes he kissed every inch of her exposed body, telling Lily he loved her, repeatedly. He gently fondled her breasts, then moved his hands slowly down her body until he reached her genital area. "Are you sure you want me, my darling?"

Lily had never experienced such intimate talk and touching. Her body was aching to be taken, and she pulled Kennedy's body to hers and pleaded with him to enter her. But he wanted her to experience foreplay, so the touching and kissing began, and Lily lay there as he caressed her, then it became too much. Her back arched and she was ready; she wanted to feel Kennedy become part of her, so she guided his manly part to where it was needed. Kennedy heard Lily whispering that this was the most beautiful feeling she had ever had. He felt pleased that he had satisfied her, as he was frightened she might remember her last experience. He was totally in love with her and would do anything that she asked of him. They lay in each other's arms, both feeling relaxed, especially Lily, as she was hoping he had sowed the seed that would make her pregnant again. Now it was time for Lily to dress, and it was only then she saw her ripped dress under his pillow.

"Why do you still have my dress?"

"Because, Lily, I could not have you, but I still had a reminder, that was until today. Now I have had you with your blessing, please come and visit me whenever you need to. You know you are my one and only love. I will wait forever."

"Oh Kennedy, you are a beautiful, caring soul and I do have feelings for you. Thank you for tonight." With these words she left his pad and drove home.

.   .   .

One month passed and Lily hadn't had her period, so she prayed she was pregnant. Her work was keeping her busy. The client that had asked her to find out if he was the father of his ex-wife's daughter had finally come back to her; she thought he had vanished from her radar. But getting a sample of the daughter's hair had proved difficult. Lily told him it would be at least a week before the lab got back to her and she would contact him when the results came through. That afternoon she drove to the lab to drop off her client's details and was met by the same young lab assistant who had helped her.

"I still have your DNA details here; would you like to take them with you?" he asked.

"No, I will pick them up next week when I come back for my client's results," she told him. She didn't really need them any more, as she knew in her own mind that Kennedy was Leila's father.

Nearly two weeks passed before the lab rang to say her client's results were there. Lily had taken a pregnancy test in the morning and it tested positive, so she was on top of the world. Reece had abstained from having sex on a friend's advice, as he had the same problem, so was told by his doctor to stop being intimate for two months and this worked for him. Lily knew for sure this was Kennedy's baby as she had visited him on more than one occasion. She was surprised that she had returned to his bed, but she felt an excitement that was new to her; was it because he made her feel special? The magic was disappearing from being bedded by Reece. She hoped it would come back once he knew she was pregnant, as she felt he had an agenda each time, that the thought of making a baby had outweighed his feelings. She decided not to say anything to Reece until they resumed being intimate again, then she would wait for one month to tell him.

Today she was at the lab picking up her client's results when the assistant handed her an envelope. "Here are your results. Please take them with you before they get lost." She put it in her bag. She would open it later, but she already knew – no surprises there, she told herself. Once she was back in her office, she decided to open her envelope before she tore it up, as she didn't want Reece to see it. On reading the results, she suddenly slumped back in her chair and the letter fell from her hand. She was in total shock! "Oh, no," she sobbed, there must be some mistake? The DNA was a match to Reece. He was Leila's biological father.

It was Friday night again and the lads were meeting to see how their crypto investment was performing. Lincoln pulled up their wallet, but there was little joy, as the bitcoin was still declining. Kennedy had been studying up on NFTs and suggested perhaps they should think about spreading their portfolio. He had been told by an investor of good repute that this digital media begins its journey on a blockchain, a decentralized digital ledger that is incorruptible and indestructible. It sounded almost foolproof, but as they knew the crypto world was volatile.

But they were young and risk-takers, as the risk they had taken on the bitcoin had turned them into millionaires, then billionaires and back to millionaires. They had a lifetime in front of them.

Kennedy tried to explain that to buy an NFT is like owning a rare coin. You are paying for a token that represents an asset. The token carries the information of the asset that proves its authenticity. The main appeal of NRTs is that they are something people can buy and speculate with. He knew of someone who had made a lot of money trading in artwork; it was the up-and-coming way to make a quick million or two. A fine example of this was the artwork of an artist named Beeple. He painted or took a photo a day for 5000 days, then put them all together on an artboard. The bidding had started off at $100 and ended up as a digital NFT sale for $69 million, which was a record price. Because there is no third party involved, the price was set between the artist and the buyer. Kennedy suggested they follow this new up-and-coming artist, as he had paved the way for his future. Lincoln said he would follow up on him and find out all the information he could. They decided to call a meeting for the following Friday night.

Lily had a dark cloud hanging over her. She was still trying to process what the DNA result yielded. Why hadn't she become pregnant for two years? It was only natural to think perhaps Reece might not be able to father children. Now she had been proved wrong! What on earth was she going to do? She needed time to work this out. Should she contact Kennedy and disappoint him? No, she couldn't do that at the moment, as her feelings for him were deepening. Now that she and Reece had resumed intimacy, it wouldn't be long before she could tell him she was pregnant. This baby was Kennedy's; there was no doubt this time. Lily's heart was heavy, what a burden to have to harbour on her own. If only she had taken the envelope when she was first offered it, she would not be in this situation. Instead, she had started a relationship with Kennedy, which was to get pregnant; it was a means to an end, with no feelings involved, but this did not turn out to be the case. Sadly, feelings did become involved!

This morning Lily felt sick so rushed to the bathroom. She knew it was morning sickness as she had experienced this while pregnant with Leila. Reece heard her so went to investigate. It was then he learned of her pregnancy. He was elated – at last it had happened, and he didn't need to go and be tested. Finally, they were having their second baby!

Reece could not wait to tell his partners that Lily was finally pregnant again. This took Kennedy by surprise, as she had not told him. He knew the baby was his, so why hadn't she been to visit him? He had to meet her and find out why. Was he now the father of her two children? Kennedy knew Reece was working late this week, so he went round to their house to speak with Lily. When she opened the door and saw Kennedy standing there she burst into tears. "I'm sorry I haven't been to see you. I don't know what to do. Please help me, Kennedy?"

"What is wrong, Lily?"

She didn't know where to start. Was this the time to tell him that Leila was not his? "I am pregnant with your baby. I had a DNA test to find out who Leila's father was. Reece is her biological father. I am sorry, Kennedy." He was as shocked as Lily was when she read the results.

"Are you sure?" he asked.

"Yes, the laboratory did the tests and Reece's DNA is a match. It does not mean you should not love her as you do, but my next baby is yours; there is no mistaking this."

He was a little disappointed to know Leila was not his little girl. He had been so convinced, as was Lily. But he was happy to know he was going to have a baby with Lily. He hoped it would be another little girl. He took Lily into his arms and begged her to come and visit him. He wanted to hold her and tell her how much he loved her. As he thought about Leila's birth, a sudden feeling of relief overcame him: she was a child born out of love, not from a night of unconsented sex, by the selfish act of one person.

A meeting was called at Lincoln's pad as he had some new information on the NFT scene. The artist that had painted 'every days' – the first 5000 days, which he had been working on since 2007 and had sold for $69 million, had new works coming up. Was he the person to invest in. Was this where their future lay? If they acted sooner rather than later, they might catch the hype before other investors woke up to the fact that here was an opening to make big money. It was a unanimous vote to spend some of their bitcoin and spread their investments in another field. It would give them a feeling of security, as the bitcoin was still declining, and they needed a boost to save their failing cryptocurrency portfolio. No one knew what was going to happen to the markets, but hopefully it would recover; it all depended on who wanted to buy and at what price.

"What do we know about this artist?" asked Reece.

Lincoln explained: "He put his art on NFTs for sale at $100 and the bidders pushed it to a record price. That's the way it works; it is up to the people themselves to set the price. Now that he has made a name for himself, people will want to follow him. He has a new work up for sale. It has a relevance to climate change, as it warns about potential catastrophes. This could be our entry into NFT trading, so if we want to act, let us do it now."

They knew it was going to cost them, and it was a gamble, but if they could secure the authentic rights then no one could reproduce it.

Kennedy, being the financial advisor, wanted to make sure it had an attached NFT licence which clearly described the rights they would own on purchasing it. "So, what are we actually buying?" asked Reece, who still hadn't grasped the NFT concept. Lincoln explained that they would be buying a link to a file, as they are digital assets and only exist in digital form; you cannot touch them. "But how do we view the art piece we have purchased?" asked Reece, still a little perplexed.

"We cannot display it in our homes, but we can see it

on screen," said Lincoln. "The main reason we are buying this is because it is a speculative investment, along with having the pleasure of something unique from an admired artist. An NFT is a digital certificate of ownership traceable on a blockchain and is a representation of art."

It was taking time for Reece to get his head around all this, as he did not have the intelligence of his two partners. "You guys are the experts, and I trust your judgement, so let's do it!"

Now that it was agreed upon, it was up to Lincoln to use his expertise. Kennedy reminded him that the creator of the work is the owner of the copyright, so they needed this assigned to them in writing from the creator. This was a safeguard, because Kennedy was the financial whizz, and nothing was going to be left to chance. They had to own it legitimately, especially with the amount of money they were going to spend. He was mindful it was Reece's money that had set them up, and if he hadn't been for their friend, they would not be where they were today. To make the investment Lincoln knew he needed cryptocurrency, which was not a worry because they had plenty. Because most of the big companies used Ethereum currency, he had to change the bitcoin into this currency. Ethereum made NFTs possible because of its blockchain, as it could hold extra information. They were already set up with a digital crypto wallet, which acted like a bank account for trading, investing and selling cryptocurrencies. Buying an NFT of a painting means you have virtually paid for a string of numbers and characters, and an NFT is essentially a tradeable jpeg or GIF.

Lincoln found the digital artwork they wanted to buy on a 'buy now' site. All he had to do was match the price that was being asked. But first he had to secure the NFT licence from the creator. Once this was agreed upon, he pushed the 'buy now' tab and the artwork was theirs. They were the proud owners of an expensive piece of digital art, and they had entered the world of NFTs. Their cryptocurrency investment had diminished somewhat with the purchase they had just made. Between their two investments, surely one was going to increase substantially in value. It was time to celebrate.

Time was getting near for Lily to have her second child. Leila was coming up three and was excited about having a new little brother or sister. Lily had been to visit Kennedy on several occasions as he wanted to feel the movements of the baby, and just to be able to put his hands on her stomach nearly brought him to his knees. She could not deny him this request. She was fighting her feelings for him, but in the end, she couldn't fight them any longer; they were there and she took comfort in the fact that this was his baby. They had talked about names and Kennedy asked that if it was a little girl whether she could be named Mackenzie. He didn't have a preference for a boy's name so left that up to Lily. Now all she had to do was suggest this to Reece and hope he had no misgivings with it. If the baby was a boy, there would be no problems with a name. Together Lily and Kennedy secretly hoped for another little girl, but only time would tell.

Lily had taken maternity leave but was keeping up with her law studies so she could keep her dreams alive to become a judge. This is what she was striving for, which meant she had to pass more degrees before reaching that milestone in her life. She wanted her family close, so she could concentrate on her career. Reece wanted three children, and this worried Lily that it might take another two years after her second birth to become pregnant again. This would be putting her career on hold longer than she would have liked.

Tonight, at home, the subject of baby names came up. Reece suggested Willow for a girl and William for a boy. It was then Lily put her spoke in. "I would like Mackenzie for a girl; you can choose a boy's name. You chose Leila, so now I would like my say."

Reece thought on this for a moment, but the name Mackenzie wasn't what he would have chosen. "Leave it with me and I will think about it," he told her. Lily hoped this wouldn't develop into an argument, as she was determined to stick with her and Kennedy's decision, and she thought he deserved to have a say.

Later that night Lily woke in terrible pain and she knew it was time to go to the hospital. They had arranged for Kennedy to be called upon as Leila loved him and wouldn't be upset to find her mother gone in the morning. Reece ran to the phone and rang Kennedy and asked him to come immediately, then rang the hospital. Meanwhile Lily put the last-minute things into her already packed bag, amid the pain that was wracking her body. Within five minutes Kennedy arrived. He took one look at Lily, who was doubled over in pain, and his heart went out to her. "I'll get the car, you stay with Lily," Reece called to Kennedy. As soon as he closed the door, Kennedy took Lily in his arms and declared his undying love for her. "I will love our baby Lily, but you will always come first in my life. This is the best present anyone could wish for, thank you, take care my love," as he kissed her goodbye.

The door opened and Reece came in and helped Lily out to the car. As they were driving to the hospital, Lily's pain became so intense she cried out to Reece to hurry. They only just made it when the baby decided to come. There was a bed in the corridor and that was as far as she got. Staff were rushing everywhere and a nurse was asking her to hold on until they reached the ward, but it all happened there. Lily was in pain then it ceased and she heard the nurse say something about a baby boy, but minutes later the pain came back and her body went into shock. She was rushed off to intensive care where they could monitor her.

Two days passed before Lily woke. All she could see were machines surrounding her and she was on her own. Where was everyone? she wondered. A nurse appeared as they had seen on the monitor that she had woken. "What happened?" Lily asked.

"You have been very sick for two days, after giving birth to twins."

"Twins! No one told me I was having twins. Are they okay?"

"Yes, you have a baby boy and a baby girl. They are tiny so will be in incubators for a few weeks."

Lily could not believe she had given birth to twins. Then reality hit her. Kennedy had fathered twins. What would he think? As she thought about it, Reece wanted three children and now they had them she hoped this was the end, as she didn't want to have to go through this ever again. Now her family was complete and so close together: how wonderful! As she tried to focus on the babies, the only thought running through her mind was Kennedy. She wanted to see him and share this special moment with him, but her first visitor would be Reece. How was she going to feel, as he would be acting the proud father? It was too much for Lily, so she closed her eyes and drifted off to sleep.

'Wake up, my darling," were the first words Lily heard as she turned over in her bed. Standing at her bedside was Reece. "What a shock you gave us, Lily. Everyone was so worried about you. Have you seen our babies? Fancy us having twins. I'm so proud."

"I haven't seen them yet; will you take me to have a peek?" Lily asked. But at the end of her bed was a sign saying she was confined to bed, so Reece had to explain this to her.

"But why?"

It was then she learned she had nearly died while giving birth, that she would be in hospital for at least a week. The babies were being looked after in the nursery by the nursing staff as she was too weak to manage them. Then she asked how Leila was as she was missing her.

"Kennedy is looking after her, at nights, so I can be here with you. He is a true friend, Lily. I don't know how we can thank him," he said with such sincerity. Just the mention of his name brought tears to her eyes. She had nearly died having his babies, did he know this? she wondered.

"Have you told Kennedy about the babies and me?" she asked. Reece said Kennedy was coming to see her tomorrow night, as he was worried, so he would stay at home with Leila, to let him visit. With this news Lily closed her eyes, she felt at peace, then tiredness took over. Reece could see she needed rest, so he gently kissed her and told her he loved her, then he left.

Today Lily was feeling a little better, although she wished she could cuddle her babies, so asked the nurse if she could go and see them. The nurse told Lily she would bring the babies to her; she was not allowed up yet, as she was still very weak. She tried to sit up in the bed, then realised why she was not allowed out, as all her energy was sapped from her body. When the babies were wheeled in, in their incubators, they were so small, and her tears flowed.

"Are they going to be alright?"

The nurse told her they were both healthy, just a little underweight, but they would catch up to normal babies in the next couple of months. As Lily looked at the tiny bundles, her mind went to Kennedy. She couldn't wait for him to see them. What would he think?

"Wake up, my darling" were the words Lily could hear as she stirred. It took a few minutes for her brain to focus and there beside her bed stood Kennedy. She tried to sit up, but her body let her down, so she just lay there. Just seeing him filled her with tears. "I'm sorry, I must look dreadful," she sobbed.

He leaned over and kissed her cheek. "What a clever girl you are giving me twins. Thank you, my darling. I know it hasn't been easy, but I will make it up to you. I will always be here for you, Lily." Just hearing these tender words from Kennedy tore at her heart.

"How is Leila?" she asked. She had to change the subject before more tears of joy flowed. He told her he loved looking after her, as he had to read her a story each night before she would settle.

"She is excited to know there are two babies coming home, not one, but two! Talking of babies, can I have a peep at my progeny?" he asked.

Lily pushed the button for the nurse to come and take Kennedy to see the twins. "They are very tiny, but they are both healthy," Lily warned him. Off he went with the nurse to the nursery and when he saw the two little bundles lying together, he was shocked to see how small they were.

"Are they going to be, okay?" he enquired.

The nurse assured him that within a couple of months they would be like any ordinary babies. "It's just that no one foresaw there were two babies, so no one was prepared," she told Kennedy.

"How can that happen?"

The nurse told him that sometimes one baby can be hidden and only one heartbeat is picked up. He was sad he couldn't hold his babies, but because they were in incubators only the parents could hold them, and he wasn't the parent to the outside world!

When he came back to the ward, Lily had put some makeup on and brushed her hair. Kennedy wanted to take her in his arms and hold her tight, but because a nurse was there, he had to restrain himself. "Oh my God, they are so tiny. You will be busy coping with three little ones, but I will come often and help you and give them plenty of cuddles," he told her.

Suddenly the nurse disappeared so he could tell Lily how he felt. "I love you, Lily, with all my heart," and he took her hand and rested it on his chest. She was touched by his tenderness; with this she knew how deep her feelings went for him. But, in reality, she had to remind herself she was married to Reece. Worse than that, she had been bedded by half-brothers, not that anyone but herself knew of this. She had so many secrets; her life was like a story book. Thank goodness no one could read it, as so many hearts would be broken.

That night on his way home from visiting Lily, Kennedy called in to see Reece, to let him know Lily was in good spirits and that he had seen the babies. Reece opened a bottle of wine to wet the babies' heads.

"And to toast your wife," added Kennedy, who was a little annoyed, as he would have toasted Lily first. During their conversation Reece brought up the subject of names. "Lily wanted to call the baby Mackenzie if it was a girl, but I can't come to terms with that name. What do you think?" he asked. Kennedy couldn't wait to have his say, "I think that is a beautiful name. Let her have the choice; she has done the hard yards, so be fair, Reece. What about a boy's name?" he asked.

"I thought about William, but now we have twins it doesn't sound right with Mackenzie," Reece replied.

"What about Harrison?"

Reece thought for a moment and churned the two names over in his mind. Yes, they sounded good together.

"Right, Harrison it is," he replied. This left Kennedy ecstatic, as now he had named both his babies.

The lads had arranged to meet on Friday, so today it had to be at Reece's home as he had Leila to look after. Lily and the babies were still in hospital. Lincoln was bringing his iPad to show the image of the digital artwork they now owned. He was happy, as this week there had been so much publicity about this new artist, so this was a real boost for them. What they had to decide was whether they would hang on to it, or if they received an offer way above what they paid, would they let it go?

"Right guys, here is our purchase," and he pulled it up on the screen. Kennedy and Reece were most impressed. There on stilts above a volume of water was a building stacked with a bus, containers, a caravan, cartons and everything else pertaining to life. This was indeed a piece of art that told a story of what would happen to our planet, if indeed climate change wasn't addressed. Could this be their cue to making millions? They had paid $2.7 million; would it be popular? Would it push the price way beyond their expectations? It was a matter of wait and see, which was the price the lads paid for taking risks. They knew with this came bragging rights, as owning a unique piece of sought-after digital art was just the hype they wanted.

Then suddenly Lincoln noticed a bid had come through for their new digital art piece, then another bid, then a counter offer by the first bidder; what was going on? They could not believe this was happening before their very eyes, right here on the screen. The highest bid at this stage was $5 million.

"What are we going to do?" asked Lincoln. Kennedy and Reece were in total disbelief, and silence reigned. "Do we sell or do we wait?" he asked again. Kennedy suggested they wait to see what eventuated overnight. There would be very little sleep had tonight, by these risk-takers.

The next morning, they gathered at Lincoln's pad. Leila was being looked after by her nanny, so this left Reece free for the day. On went the computer and three eager beavers peered at the screen, not knowing what to expect. A new bid had reached $9 million; was this the winning bid? It was time for them to make a crucial decision. Would they hang out for a higher price and risk losing the present bid, or would they push the 'sell' button?

"Let's make a decision right now," said a determined Lincoln. It was decided unanimously that they push the 'sell' button. Lincoln released the NFT licence to the new owner. It was unbelievable that they had bought at $2.7 million and sold for $9 million in a matter of two weeks.

"How easy was that?" remarked Lincoln.

Over the next week there was a lot of criticism in the media about the cryptocurrency world. Things like … a dangerous cult, crypto meltdown, get-rich-quick scheme, unregulated market, buying in a dip just a disaster, an unpredictable market … but in today's world, what was a predictable market? Scams were also mentioned, but one had to remember there were scams everywhere, in all parts of everyday life, not just in the crypto world. The picture painted by news outlets left a dim overall view on this subject. The lads were uncomfortable with all this negative hype. In the investment sector no one could be sure where to invest money and feel safe. It was with the risk takers that fortune favoured the brave! It was the world of the young 'fly-by-the-seat-of your-pants' guys, the adrenaline junkies, but certainly not a landscape for the faint-hearted.

The day had arrived for Lily and the twins to come home. Reece had been out doubling up on the already bought baby gear, as now they needed two of everything. The single pushchair was exchanged for a double buggy and a second bassinette was purchased. Lily's health was nearly back to normal, but it was going to be a strain on her to manage the twins and Leila, although she had the nanny during the day. The lads were there to welcome the extended family home, with one especially who couldn't wait to hold his babies, as these little bundles of joy were conceived during nights of passion with the love of his life. Both Lincoln and Kennedy were given a twin to hold, while Reece and Lily made up the bassinettes.

While Mackenzie lay in Kennedy's arms, he felt a warmth coming from this tiny bundle of joy; was this because he was her biological father? He was a natural with babies as he had been in Leila's company since she was a baby. But poor Lincoln, he felt like a fish out of water. He had not held a baby before, so he hoped he could hand him back, sooner rather than later. He was a computer geek; babies weren't on his radar any time soon. He watched Kennedy talking away to baby Mackenzie, which totally amazed him. His thoughts led him to believe he would make a wonderful father, but then came the worry: why had he stopped dating? This was a total mystery to everyone, as he and Reece had had many chats about Kennedy's lack of interest in the opposite sex, especially knowing he was once the playboy of the group. Both had approached Kennedy on this subject. Perhaps now was the right time to try again? "You are so relaxed with little ones, Kennedy; you should have children of your own. Find yourself a partner and settle down. You are not getting any younger," Lincoln commented. Lily turned around to hear Kennedy's answer, when suddenly their eyes met, with neither wanting to look away. To an observant person, there lay the answer!

"I'm in no hurry. I love this family, and their children are my children," he replied. This answer seemed to satisfy the status quo for the moment, as that conversation ended right there. Lily's heart warmed; she thought he had answered in a caring, loving way, that only she could feel, as it must be sad for him to know that his babies were going to be brought up in Reece's name. She did quietly wonder how this was all going to pan out, but that was a long way off. All she had time for, in the following months, were her two little babies.

The investment world

Lincoln's interest was drawn to an article in the business section of the local newspaper. It read: 'The next generation of punters want access to new asset classes. Crypto was stirring in the minds of the young investors, and it had established itself as a legitimate asset class.' Then it continued to say that crypto could be risky, but as Lincoln knew, what investment didn't come under that same umbrella, as today, in this unsettled environment, even life was a gamble. What was it with the crypto world that put it in the limelight? Was it not understood, or was it because it was unregulated? To the banks, it was enemy number one!

It was time for Lincoln to see what NFTs digital art was flourishing on the computer, as the lads were coming tomorrow night to see what was available for sale. Now they had been bitten by the NFTs bug, they were eager to repeat their good luck. Their bitcoin wallet was still on a downhill slide, and it had lost half its value, but by the grace of God, the profit from the sale of the digital art was able to top it up. He wasn't sure if they should stick with the same art creator, as there were new pieces of art being displayed that were also bringing record prices. He would leave it up to the lads to make a decision when they arrived. Was their good luck going to continue? Were they riding the crest of another wave?

The lads were gathered at their arranged meeting, eager to see what digital art Lincoln had picked for them to look at. First viewed was a piece by the same artist as their first purchase and it was a video clip, showing a former US president lying naked on the ground, covered in graffiti. The second piece was of 'Cryptokitty', which was a series of cartoon kittens.

"Why would someone pay such big money for a digital token of a collectable cat?" asked Reece.

"You just need to look at the prices they are selling for, so what we have to gamble on is whether they go higher. Could they reach the million-dollar mark?" said Kennedy.

Lincoln was favouring the first option. They knew this artist, it was this one who had made them the big money, so why change, he thought to himself.

"Look guys, the creator of the world's most expensive NFT art, which was a mixture of drawings, photography and digital renderings, were compiled into one single piece. I worked out that each piece was worth $13,860, not a bad day's work. See, topics are important, as it was associated with political and cultural events. Christies had it as an NFT jpeg file, bidding was set at $100 and the rest was history. I think this must be the creator to follow, as people have become more interested in what is happening around them, and this guy knows this, hence his good fortune."

"You are right, Lincoln. I agree, let's go with this man; he has been good to us. Are you with us, Reece?" Kennedy asked. This was not Reece's field, so he went along with the status quo, as he trusted his friends' decisions. This was all new territory to him and he was still finding it hard to fully grasp the concept of NFTs. "What do you think has made this trend towards NFTs virtual art?" he asked.

Kennedy had noticed at his workplace that many of his co-workers were working from home because of the Covid outbreak, so most of their socializing was done through a screen. He didn't think it would be long before people turned to living life virtually, so why not the art markets too? Gone would be the days of storage and handling, which was an extra expense. Virtual crypto art took up no room in homes as it was not able to be displayed, and the only space it is stored is on a computer.

"I cannot come to terms with the fact that people are happy to store their art in a computer and not hanging on a wall," Reece said. "I like to look at and admire my purchases. In my hotel, if I didn't have art on display, what would people look at? Not only is it eye-catching, but it can be a point of conversation. Really guys, this concept is not easy for me to understand. Surely NFTs must have doubters; there must be people out there that think like me? What will happen if the upward trend of NFTs in the art industry continues? Will we be re-evaluating the meaning of art itself? Walls would look bare, and what would take art's place? It frightens me, that is why I am fighting with my understanding of the value of digital art."

Reece's workplace was so different to that of his crypto partners. They used their brainpower whereas he used his outgoing personality. Their life interests were similar, but Kennedy's and Lincoln's brainpower had helped them to become millionaires, so who was he to question his partners decisions? he asked himself. The decision was made to go with their original artist, as they knew he was a safe bet and he had already proved his worth. Once again it was Lincoln's computer skills that came to the fore, as he exchanged bitcoin for Ethereum cryptocurrency. Buying NFTs artwork allowed them to speculate and hopefully repeat their last windfall. This was using up more of their bitcoin investment, but it was not performing to their expectations!

Lily's life was jammed full looking after the twins and Leila. She had no time to think about her love life; that would come later. Kennedy was spending more time than usual at their home, as he wanted to be there and help bring up his children. Reece didn't seem to notice his increased visits as he was working long hours and it just meant he didn't have to spend so much time with the children when he came home exhausted. Covid had taken its toll on many of his staff, so he was filling in anywhere he was needed.

Lily enjoyed having Kennedy's company, and he was a hands-on-dad and loved all three children. He was happy being in Lily's presence, as his feeling were as strong as ever. He couldn't wait for her to find time to become his lover again, but he knew the children had to come first, and his time would come soon enough. Leila had now started day-care, so each lunch break he would come around and spend time with Mackenzie and Harrison. He marvelled at how well they were doing, as they were now on a par with babies their own age. At the weekends he spent a lot of time with the twins.

A stranger calls

One evening while at home Kennedy received a phone call from a lady who said she was his mother and wanted to meet up with him. This was the first contact between mother and son in fifteen years, so he felt a little apprehensive; why was she suddenly wanting to see him? He agreed to meet her the following lunch hour at a café, as she was staying in his home town. Today he would miss seeing his babies, but he was puzzled as to why after all these years this person wanted to meet him. Over the years, he had told himself she was never going to be part of his life, but when he was confronted, blood seemed to be thicker than water. Now that he was a parent himself his mind-set had changed on a lot of matters, and he knew family connection was a vital part of everyone's life.

As Kennedy entered the café, he looked around to see

if he could pick out his mother, but no one seemed to fill his expectations. He ordered a coffee and went to a table to wait, but no one approached him. Ten minutes passed and still he was on his own. Just as he was about to leave, a thin frail lady came to him and asked if he was Kennedy. He went into total shock, as this person looked very sick. Surely she wasn't his mother?

"I'm so sorry for being a terrible mother, but I never forgot you and your sister. You deserved better; I have made a mess of my life, but I just had to see you before I go."

These words left him stunned. "What do you mean?" he asked.

"I am terminally ill and I don't have long," she answered and it was then he noticed tears running down her cheeks. Kennedy's heart was broken, he went to her and took her in his arms.

"I'm so sorry, I'm so sorry" she kept muttering over and over between her sobs.

Suddenly he felt a connection with this lonely soul. "It's alright, Mother, I'm here," he whispered in her ear. "Come home with me and we can talk. We have so many lost years to catch up on," he told her. With this he walked her out to his car and drove home.

Kennedy listened as his mother told of her mixed-up life and the heartaches that accompanied the wrong decisions she had made. She had left his father for another man, they had twins, a boy and a girl, and when they were six, she walked out on her responsibilities. She didn't know what happened to the twins as she was not allowed to have contact with them. From then on, she drifted in and out of abusive relationships and now she had no one and very little money. She was destitute and terminally ill.

Kennedy could not believe that someone so close to him had endured such sadness. "Where are you staying, Mother?" he asked. When she told him she was staying in a homeless shelter, he was in shock. "You will come and stay with me. We will go and pick up your belongings after we have eaten." With this he began preparing something for them to eat. He was good at rattling up a meal from virtually nothing, which was what bachelors did.

"What about yourself, Kennedy, are you married?" she asked. He explained he was still single.

"But you are a nice-looking young man. Why haven't you found anyone?"

Kennedy could have elaborated on this, but tonight wasn't the time. Then she asked what line of work he was in. "Dad put us through university and I studied finance, so now I am a financial advisor for a large company. I have been lucky with my life as opportunities have come my way. If my friend's parents weren't killed in a plane crash in Australia, then it could have been a lot different. Along with my two best friends we have prospered."

It was then she asked how his father was. "Dad never married again after you left; he was a bitter man. Because he looked after me, I made a promise to myself to care for him in his old age and that is what I am doing."

After they had eaten, Kennedy suggested they drive and pick up his mother's belongings. He would never forgive himself if he left her to stay in a homeless shelter when she was so ill. He pulled up in front of an old building in which she said she was staying. She told him to stay in the car until she came back. He watched on with great sadness as she slowly made her way up the path. Kennedy was still trying to take in all he had been told; what a sad life, and she had no purpose to carry on and live for. There didn't appear to be any highlights in her miserable existence.

He saw her come out the door, so he got out of the car and walked towards her. "I'll take this, Mother. You go and get the rest of your belongings."

"This is all I have, son."

He stopped in total disbelief; was this all she owned after a lifetime? He could not hold back. "Please, Mother, don't worry any more. I will look after you," he said, as he fought to hold back his tears. He took her hand and led her back to his car. "You can stay with me. I only have a bachelor pad, but we will go and find a nice house. I need a bigger home for when the babies come and stay."

"What babies?" she asked.

He told her it was a long story; he would tell her another day.

"Thank you, son, it won't be for long," she whispered. Kennedy could see she was in need of rest, so he drove straight home. He settled her into a chair while he went to his bedroom and whipped the sheets off the bed and swapped them for clean ones. This would be where she slept tonight.

As Kennedy lay huddled up on the settee, he thought through the day's happenings. He felt weighed down by the fact that his mother was homeless. What would have happened to her if she hadn't made contact with him; would she have died a pauper? This thought brought more tears – to be so alone in her old age with death knocking on her door. Then there were his half-brother and sister; where were they?

Suddenly it dawned on him there were twins in his family; his mother's genes must have passed down to him, as he had fathered twins. She hadn't asked about his sister; she was living in Canada and he kept in touch with her through his father. How was he going to tell his father about his mother's return, as he had carried the bitterness through all these years. Would he relent and feel sorry for her? Regardless of his decision, she was still his mother and he felt he had a duty to care for her, especially now that she was terminally ill.

His thoughts were disturbed by a terrible bout of coughing coming from the bedroom. He listened, but it was too much so he jumped up and went to the bedroom door.

"Are you alright, Mother?"

"It's okay, son, I need some medicine, but I have no money. I'll be fine."

"Try to get some sleep. I will take you to the doctor tomorrow and we will get you what you need."

He heard her say in a quiet voice, "You're a good boy, Kennedy."

The next morning, he was woken by the phone ringing. It took him a minute or two to work out why he was lying on the settee, then it all came flooding back. "Hi, Kennedy, you didn't come to see the twins yesterday. We missed you. Leila cried because you weren't here to give her a hug. Are you okay?" asked Lily.

Where would he start? "I'm fine, my darling. My mother is staying with me. It is a long story, so I won't be there today either as I am taking her to see a doctor. She isn't well."

Lily told him they would miss him, to call her when convenient. As Kennedy was preparing breakfast his mother appeared at the door. She looked terrible, her eyes were red and she was staggery on her feet. "Mother, what is wrong?" he asked, as he went to help her.

"Please, son, take me to a doctor, I need some medicine!" He asked her to have a little something to eat, but she insisted she had to get to a doctor. Kennedy helped her out to the car then drove to the nearest medical centre. The doctor on call asked them to come into his surgery. He took one look at the patient and knew immediately she was very sick. "What is wrong, my dear?" he asked.

"I have cancer and there is nothing more that can be done for me. I am dying. I need painkillers. Please help me." When the doctor asked her what medication she was on, he was shocked to learn she wasn't taking any, because she had no money. He looked directly at Kennedy, so he told the doctor her story.

"Here my dear, take this now," and he gave her a capsule to swallow. He then asked her how long she had.

"I only have a month, six weeks at the most," she replied. He then told her he would give her a bottle of capsules, of which she must take one every two hours to keep the pain at bay. He wrote out a prescription for some sleeping pills and told her to rest, as that was best for her. "Come back next Thursday and see me. Take care, my dear," he told her.

Kennedy's pad was not the place he wanted her to spend her short time left, and he had thought about a larger home but had been putting it off. Now, though, was the time to do something. He called Lily to see if she could come with him to help choose a place where his mother would be happy. The nanny could look after the children for a couple of hours, as Reece was busy at work. He would get his mother settled in bed so she could rest, then he would pick Lily up.

He had called a real-estate friend to see what houses he had that they could move into straight away. He had two nice homes with lovely gardens so arranged to meet Kennedy at the given address. As he and Lily inspected the two homes, they both liked the same one so that was easily settled. He shook the agent's hand and the deal was done, so it was arranged that they move in at the weekend.

As they were driving home Lily asked if she could meet Kennedy's mother, so he drove back to his pad. He had to warn her that she was very sick, not to be shocked by her appearance. Before they alighted from the car Kennedy leaned over and kissed her on the cheek, then took her hand and placed it on his heart. This was something he always did; it was his way of telling her his heart belonged to her. As they entered his pad, he called to his mother to come and meet a friend, but there was no answer, so he rushed into her bedroom only to find her curled up in a ball, sobbing her heart out.

"What is wrong, Mother?" he asked as he lifted her up and held her.

"I will only know you for a short time. You seem such a nice young man, but I will never really get to know you," she sobbed.

"I will take time off work and we will do things together. Mother, meet Lily; she is my best friend."

With this Lily came over and took her hand. "You have a wonderful son. He is so caring. He will tell you a secret that will make you happy," she told her. Then a terrible feeling came over her. Here was Kennedy and Reece's mother and Lily was the only one that knew this. She had children to the two half-brothers; God forbid if this ever got out!

That night after they had tea Kennedy sat with his mother and told her about his babies. Although Lily was married to his best friend, the twins were his. "It's so complicated, I can't go into details, but you are a grandmother. Lily's husband doesn't know they are my twins so we have to keep it a secret."

Suddenly he saw her smiling. "When can I see my grandchildren?" she asked.

Kennedy told her they were shifting at the weekend so it would be after that. "You will have a nice garden to sit in and listen to the birds, it will be peaceful, you will love it," he told her.

"You know, son, I have never had a nice house. I lived in rented places all my life and some were pretty rough, times were tough, but I managed to survive."

It was all go. Lincoln had come to help with the shift, as Reece was busy at work. He decided only to take what he needed, as he would buy new furniture. His old stuff would look out of place in his new home. Lily had chosen a bedroom suite and some nice feminine linen and nightwear, as virtually all his mother owned was what she was standing in. She also brought her some clothes as she was too sick to do any shopping.

When his mother saw where she was going to live, she was so happy, as this was her last resting place. She had never had such luxury and to think it had arrived as her life was nearing the end. Everyone knew she was dying so they tried to create a happy atmosphere. Kennedy would deal to his bachelor pad once his mother was gone. Today it was back to the doctor for their appointment.

"How are you today, my dear?" he asked.

She told him the pain was mostly under control, but he noticed her eyes were sunken and had dark circles around them. He knew her time was near, so he called Kennedy into another room and made him aware of this. He prescribed her a larger dose of morphine to be taken when needed.

Today Lily was bringing the twins to visit their grandmother, not that they were old enough to know her. The moment she saw them she burst into tears. She wanted to hold them as they were her son's babies, her grandchildren. Mackenzie and Harrison were now six months old. She held them one at a time and rocked them in her arms.

"You are so beautiful," she whispered to each one.

While they were all occupied, they didn't notice a car pull up the driveway. Out climbed Kennedy's father, as he knew he had brought a new home so decided to visit. "Hi, everyone," he called out. When Kennedy looked up and saw his father, he nearly died, as he had not told him that his mother was staying. His father came over to the group and greeted Lily and the babies then he paused and looked at the other person. It took him a moment to realise it was his ex-wife. He was shocked; she looked so old. He remembered her as a good-looking lady when he last saw her. What had happened?

"Dad, I'm sorry I haven't told you that Mother is staying with me. She is very ill and only has a little time left. She is staying with me until the end. Please don't be upset," he pleaded.

His father was speechless and could not believe what he was hearing. All the years he had been on his own, thinking she was leading the good life, but to see her today in this state left him in total disbelief. The only feelings he had was pity, pity for who she was now. No one spoke; it was an awkward moment or two for all.

"What do you think of our grandchildren?" she asked him.

He hesitated. "What grandchildren?" he asked. Things were going from bad to worse as he had not been told of Kennedy's involvement with Lily.

"These little babies are Kennedy's," she replied.

"Dad, come with me. I have to talk to you," said Kennedy, and with this he led his father to a place where they could talk in private. He had wanted to tell his father he was a grandad, but the time never seemed to be right, so now was the time, whether it was right or not.

After having been brought up to date, Kennedy's father could not believe that his son and his best friend's wife were having an affair. "You know, son, Reece's money got you to where you are today. How could you do this to him? What happens if he finds out he is not the twins' father? You have entered dangerous territory, my lad. I am disappointed this has happened. Now on to your mother. She looks like an old lady; I cannot believe that is her," he said.

"Dad, she is dying. She asked me to meet her. I rescued her from a homeless shelter. All she had was an overnight bag. What could I do? I'm going to look after her and make her life as comfortable as I can," he declared.

"You do have some good in you, son. You will do her proud. I'll go now. Today has been a shock for me, but I'll come back when I have calmed down, perhaps tomorrow," and with these words Kennedy's father left.

Holding the twins had brought back memories to Kennedy's mother of her own twins. Then the guilt started. "You know, Lily, I had twins, a boy and a girl, and I walked out on them when they were six years old. I don't know where they are or anything about them. Maybe one day Kennedy might try to find them, after I am gone."

The day came and went with a lot of truths uncovered, some happy, others sad.

Kennedy's father left feeling let down by his son and his ex-wife. All those years had passed and his bitterness had never left him. He could never form another relationship for fear of being let down once again. She was his childhood sweetheart, and although she had walked out on him several times, he never expected her to leave her children. Now he had a new worry, that of his son and Reece's wife. Why did he do this to his best friend? Sadly, no one knew why the twins were fathered by Kennedy, as there was an explanation, which at the time seemed logical! He was trying to come to terms with it all, and whether he could find a little forgiveness in his heart to visit his ex-wife. She was ill and dying, so surely this was the turning point for him. Could he let the past be forgotten and move forward? He would sleep on this thought.

The next morning, he picked up his phone and called Kennedy. "Would it be okay for me to bring a takeaway dinner around tonight?"

"You do know Mother will be here?"

"Yes, I realise that, son. I will bring enough for three."

This was a huge surprise to Kennedy. Had his father

relented at last? It was not before time, as he himself was growing old. Was this a final family farewell?

Kennedy took his mother for a drive, but she was only in the car for an hour then she asked to go home as she was in pain. He looked across at her and she had slumped down in her seat. He drove straight home, then put her to bed so she could rest up for tonight. He wondered how the night would go, with both his mother and father in the same room. Surely his father would go easy on her and leave the past behind? Only time would tell.

Leila was happy to see Kennedy again; she had not seen him for a couple of days, as she was at daycare. Reece was at home so he was able to catch up with Kennedy. "I must come and meet your mother. Lily told me she was really ill," he said.

"Yes, she only has a short time, and the day is getting nearer. Come around on Saturday morning, the sooner the better, as I don't know if she will be with us beyond the weekend," Kennedy replied. They then went on to discuss their new NFTs artwork. They had put it up for auction and neither knew how the bidding was going, but tomorrow they would find out, as Lincoln had called a meeting. Reece was keen to know if they had made the right investment, as he was still coming to terms with the NFTs. They were still way beyond his comprehension. Kennedy asked Reece how his hotel was going. "I haven't told Lily yet, but I have been offered the manager's job of a new hotel in Auckland that the company has just purchased. I don't know whether she will be happy, but it is a wonderful promotion for me. It shows that the company has faith in my ability as a manager."

This was the worst news possible for Kennedy. If they had to shift away, he would not be able to see his babies, and what of Lily? He could not survive knowing she was living elsewhere. "But, Reece, we have been friends for a long time, what would we do without you?" he asked.

"You and Lincoln can make the decisions. I am not as computer literate as you guys, not with cryptocurrencies and NFTs; they are way above me."

Kennedy asked when this move would happen and was relieved that it would not be for a couple of months, which gave him some leeway to work something out with Lily.

The next day they were huddled around Lincoln's computer waiting to see how the bidding was going on their digital art. Hopefully there was a good bid waiting. The piece had cost them $2 million. All eyes were glued to the screen, then it appeared, a bid of $7.5 million was the latest one and it still had three days to go on the auction. Yells of delight rang out from the room, but they had to decide: would they end the bidding there and accept the last bid or would they let it run its course? Lincoln made the decision to take the $7.5 million bid, his theory being 'be happy with what your gut feeling tells you'. He was after all the computer whizz and this was endorsed by Kennedy, the financial advisor. The digital world of NFTs was riding the crest of the wave, but for how long?

Lincoln did wonder if they were purchased for their perceived importance, rather than to own the asset. Was this a status symbol for the elite with plenty of money? Were they wanting to impress in a trend that was rocketing up in the crypto ladder? The bitcoin currency was slowing down whereas the NFTs were on a high. Could the lads risk another digital art purchase? They decided to leave it for a week, then meet again next Friday.

A shock revelation

Today was Saturday and Reece was coming around to meet Kennedy's mother. Kennedy sat her on the settee and covered her with a blanket as she was feeling shivery. He brushed her hair as this had become a burden for her; her arms were weak and she struggled to lift the hairbrush to her head. When he heard Reece's car pull up, he went to the door to warn him that she was failing fast.

As they came into the room, Kennedy went to introduce Reece to his mother, and she just stared at him then started to cry. "Peter, you have come to say goodbye," she sobbed. "No, Mother, this is Reece, my friend."

"No, it's Peter. I never forgot him," she was adamant.

"Who is Peter?" asked Kennedy.

"Peter worked with me at the department store," she replied. "I loved him, I got pregnant and he left me," she whispered.

"But Reece is my age, Peter would have been your age, Mother."

"He is Peter's double; he must be his son, the baby I gave up for adoption. This makes you my son," she said earnestly.

Kennedy was so embarrassed by his mother's assumption, he apologised to Reece.

"How old are you, Reece?" she asked.

When he told her the year he was born, that was the end. "That is the very year I had a baby boy. You are my son. Come here and hold my hand. I have found my lost son," she sobbed.

Reece and Kennedy just stood and stared at each other. Reece had never told Kennedy he was adopted, so this didn't make any sense to him. Reece went over and sat on the settee and held her hand. Was this his biological mother? He had no information, because his parents had died before he knew he was adopted.

"Your father came to work in the department store where I worked and we had an affair. When he found out I was pregnant he left me. I went away and had my baby, then I came back to Kennedy's father. I never told him about the baby, so he didn't know. You and Kennedy are half-brothers, that means your children are cousins."

Reece squeezed her hand to let her know he understood, then she relaxed and closed her eyes.

Kennedy was left reeling; what was that all about? Reece's parents were killed in a plane crash. He was sure his mother was delirious. As Reece stood up, Kennedy was full of apologies. He didn't understand some of the things his mother said. How could the children be cousins?

"I'll go now. I think she has dropped off to sleep, and she needs to rest," said Reece.

Kennedy apologised again to Reece.

As soon as Reece climbed into his car, he took a deep breath and closed his eyes. He asked himself if there was any truth in what she had said; was he in fact Kennedy's half-brother? But what did she mean when she said the children were cousins? Kennedy didn't have any children. He was confused, and if this was his mother, then sadly he had met her nearing the end of her life.

When Reece arrived home, he asked Lily to come and sit with him. He told her what had happened at Kennedy's home. He was still getting over the fact that perhaps he had just met his mother. This left Lily in a precarious situation as she knew the truth, that they were indeed half-brothers, but she could not let on to Reece, as then the question of the DNA tests may well arise.

"Poor Kennedy thought she was delirious, as I have never told him that I was adopted. But she said something strange that made no sense. She said the children were cousins. Kennedy doesn't have any children, so what would she mean?" he asked Lily. She had to turn away for fear her betrayal showed on her face. This was the closest yet to the truth between her and Kennedy.

"Perhaps she was a little delirious and got her facts muddled. Remember she is very ill."

When Reece left for work, as he was working the night shift, Lily called Kennedy to see if he could come around to her home. She wanted to talk to him about Reece's promotion.

"I'll get Mother into bed and settled then I will come for a quick visit, as I don't like to leave her on her own. She was a bit delirious when she met Reece. She thought he was the baby she had given up for adoption before she met my father. It was so embarrassing; I knew Reece's parents before they perished in the plane. I don't know what came over her. She seemed to think he was a younger version of her then lover. Poor Reece, he must have wondered what struck him as he left soon after. I'll see you as soon as Mother is settled."

He went to her room to make sure she was in bed. She tried telling him again that Reece was his half-brother.

"But, Mother, I have met his parents, and they perished in a plane crash in Australia last year."

"Kennedy, I know he is Peter's son. My heart is telling me so, and when I held his hand, I felt a connection. Please tell him I would like to speak with him tomorrow, as my time is near."

Kennedy told her to rest and he would pass her message on to Reece.

Lily was waiting patiently for Kennedy to arrive. She had to talk to him; how were they going to handle Reece's promotion? The twins would be separated from their father, and she would lose contact with him. It was enough to break her heart. She knew how much Kennedy loved the children and her. What was going to happen?

By the time he arrived the children were in bed, so she

had him to herself. "Has Reece told you about his promotion?" she asked.

"Yes, he told me. It left me in shock. I couldn't live without you and my babies. You are my life. Please don't leave me, Lily," he pleaded.

On hearing this, Lily burst into tears and clung to him. Could she maintain living a double life or was it all going to fall apart? She was the only one apart from Kennedy's mother that knew the truth about the half-brothers. Kennedy and Reece were the innocent parties. She wondered if she should tell him that Reece was adopted, then he might realise there was truth in his mother's words. But something stopped her from doing this.

They consoled each other as they thought of the hopelessness of the up-and-coming situation. "You know, Kennedy, Reece thinks he is not quite as smart as you and Lincoln. It is as if he wants to prove himself," sobbed Lily.

Kennedy replied: "He couldn't understand why he never inherited his parents' intelligence as they were both academic people, but they loved him for who he was, as we did. This really bugged him, and often he referred to this thinking that he was of ordinary intelligence, when they were of extraordinary intelligence. He felt at times they might have been disappointed with him, but that was far from the truth; they loved him dearly. It was through friends of theirs that he got his first job, as they owned a high-class hotel and offered him a bellboy job. From there he has worked his way up to the position as manager. They recognised his easy connection with people and his outgoing personality. That's why the hospitality industry is his calling. He doesn't have to prove himself to anyone. It's just that Lincoln and I are academics, we are nerds; he is the normal one among us."

"Thank you for your kind words. That's what I love about you, Kennedy, you speak things as they are, and there is no camouflage," said a grateful Lily.

"Something Mother said has just come to my mind. She said the children were cousins. How can that be? Reece and I are not related. She has been so mixed up lately. She has asked to see Reece tomorrow; I don't know whether I will tell him."

Lily told Kennedy he must respect his mother's dying wishes, as she knew that she was Reece's biological mother. Perhaps she wanted to tell him something before she passed away, and this would be her last chance? She wondered how all this would pan out. If the truth was ever revealed, she would be classed as 'the scarlet woman' having had babies fathered by half-brothers.

Today Reece was back at Kennedy's home as Kennedy's mother had requested. Kennedy was asked to leave the room. He was a little put out by this, but then he remembered Lily's words, 'He must respect her dying wishes'.

"Come here and sit by me, Reece. Please tell me if you know you are adopted."

Reece told her he only found out after his parents perished, and apart from that he knew nothing.

"I knew you were my son; you look so much like your father. He wasn't an academic person; he worked behind the counter in a department store, but everyone loved him. I didn't know him for long as he came from another area, but I had an affair with him, but sadly it was just a fling for him as he moved on. I'm not sure whether he knew about you. His name was Peter Wilkinson and he came from Lumsden, should you ever want to find him. Kennedy obviously doesn't know you were adopted, so I will leave it up to you to pass this information on to him. I worry about the children; what are they going to think when they find out?"

What did she mean by this statement? Reece was stunned. If this was his mother then Kennedy was his half-brother. Did this explain why he wasn't an academic? His father worked behind the counter in a department store. His head was spinning as he tried to take it all in. What was he meant to say to this person if she was his biological mother?

It was as if she knew what he was thinking, "Don't say anything, son, I'm sorry for what I did but you were better off without me. Hold my hand and call Kennedy in," she whispered. Her voice had become shaky, so he called for Kennedy. As he entered, she asked him to sit with her. It was then she uttered her last words, "I love you both."

Kennedy looked at Reece. Why did she say that? But then he thought she had lost it and wasn't responsible for what she was saying. "I'm sorry, Reece, if this has been embarrassing for you. Was she still insistent that you were her lost son?" he asked.

Reece nodded in acknowledgement. It was all over. His mother had passed away. He let her hand go and patted Kennedy on the back and signalled he was leaving. It was not the appropriate time to say what he wanted to, as Kennedy had to have time to grieve on his own and he wanted to do the same. Now he knew Kennedy was his half-brother he still had to digest it. It was hard for him to switch from having a good friend to having a half-brother. He wondered how Kennedy would accept this news and how would it affect their friendship.

Kennedy remained at his mother's bedside and held her hand. She looked so peaceful. He was happy she had a warm home and his love for her final days. This gave him some comfort. He would make sure she had a dignified burial and a nice headstone, that was the way he wanted to remember her. He would not expect his father to pay for any costs as his bitterness was still apparent, although he had made an effort to visit on several occasions.

A quiet funeral was held and everyone attended. Kennedy hadn't seen Lily for several days or his children, so the moment he set eyes on her, his feelings ran wild. His love for her was what kept him going. He couldn't understand why Reece had shed tears; why did it affect him so much? She was a total stranger, and he had only met her twice. He hoped what she rambled on about him being her lost son hadn't brought on this sadness. To see Lily crying was understandable as his mother was their children's grandmother.

Little did he know the full implications of Lily's tears. This death had brought home to her that she had lost both Reece's and Kennedy's mother and that her three children shared the same grandmother. She was the only one that knew this sordid truth, but how long could it stay that way?

Kennedy's thoughts went back to his mother, who was now in her final resting place, and she had found her peace at last. His mind would not let go of the story she told him about her sad misused life, her wasted years and her failure to settle and be a mother to her children. What of the other children, where were they? They didn't know their mother had passed away; did they even care? Sadness set in again, and he hoped it would go away. He had done his best with the little time he had with her. He knew in his heart one day he would look for his half siblings, but now his emotions were still raw.

Reece and Lily had discussed whether to tell Kennedy about Reece's adoption, but they decided to wait, as it was too soon; he was still hurting. In Reece's heart his adopted parents were who he knew and loved and for this stranger to turn up, and lay claim to him, left him unsettled and sad at the same time. "You know, Lily, I still can't get my head around the fact that my mother and father were not my biological family. They gave me everything a kid growing up could wish for, then to leave me their total wealth just blows my mind. The only reservation I had was that I wasn't a brainy child, but now I know why, as my biological father worked in a department store as a salesperson," he sighed, and Lily could see the disappointment in his face.

"Please, Reece, don't let this be a burden hanging over you. You have talent in other areas, so don't keep comparing yourself with Lincoln and Kennedy. You are being unfair to yourself. Remember who made it possible for them to become millionaires?" This was the big difference between her two lovers: one had a positive outlook while the other hadn't come to terms with his lesser intelligence. She hoped the time would not come when she had to make a choice.

Two weeks had passed and there had been no business meeting between the lads, but today was the day. They had put all their sadness behind them, so now it was time to move on. Lincoln had surfed the net and had several digital artworks for them to discuss. But first they asked him to open their wallet so they could see what their bitcoin currency was doing. This brought a smile to their faces as it was trending upwards. Had the downhill slide ceased? This gave them heart once again. They were in the cryptocurrency scene to make their fortune, not to see it disappear. Now it was on to the digital NFTs.

They had been out of the market for two weeks, so it was like starting all over again. Decisions had to be made, to stick with their original artist or take a punt on an unknown one? Much discussion was had. Reece remained quiet as he felt the other lads knew more than him – they were the intelligent ones.

"Come on, Reece, we need your feedback. What do you think?" asked Kennedy.

"I'll go along with your decisions. You are both into it. I'm just a newcomer to the crypto world, and the NFTs are taking me longer to understand but I'll get there hopefully."

Kennedy felt Reece had to be included in a decision, as it was his parents' wealth that allowed them to buy into this crazy world. "Lincoln wants to go with the original artist, but I want to go with a complete newbie. You make the decision and we will go with that," said Kennedy.

"No guys, that is putting the pressure on me. I'll go with whatever," he replied. They knew not to push Reece outside his comfort zone, as he was not as decisive as them, so it was more debating on which way to go. They studied the art and what it was fetching, then a decision was made. Because their original creator's artwork was getting very expensive to buy, they went with Kennedy's choice and decided to take a punt. Two weeks was the bidding timetable until it closed. This was going to be very interesting! They outlaid $500,000, as they felt this could be a risk that may not pay off, so they only spent what they were prepared to lose. In all, their overall financial situation had not quite reached the goal they had set themselves. When it did, there would be some more hard decisions to be made.

Reece's time was drawing near as to whether he took his new management position, so a decision had to be made. He had tried to talk to Lily about it, but she kept putting it off. "I don't want to move the children and I have a job that I love; there is just too much against us moving," she told him. He told her it was his chance to move up in the management scene and that he would feel better about himself.

"That is what it is all about; you trying to prove yourself. You don't have to do that, Reece; we love you the way you are," Lily explained. But Reece was not convinced. He felt this was his big break. With this Lily ended the discussion, as she could see this conversation wasn't going anywhere and if it didn't end here, it would turn into an argument. She just could not bring herself to up and move, as there was too much at stake. Her feelings for Kennedy were strong; in fact they surpassed how she felt about Reece. He had more to do with the children than Reece, he interacted with them, and they loved him. Reece was spending more time at work filling in for those absent with Covid, so when he came home, he was past wanting to play with the family.

Leila was at play-centre in the afternoons. She had finished the morning sessions and she told her mother she was a big girl now. The nanny looked after the twins, so Lily was back at work. She loved the interaction with her clients; it took her brain outside the family situation. On the odd occasion she would take time off work and go to Kennedy's home, an arrangement they both looked forward to. Lily loved the attention Kennedy paid her; this was missing from her marriage. Their love making excited her, as she loved the caressing and the build-up, something Reece didn't have time for, as he always had other things to attend to.

Lily was busy at work today. The gentleman who she had to get the DNA evidence for found out he was the biological father of his daughter and therefore he was pushing for part custody, much to his ex-wife's anger. She was upset when she knew he had gone to the trouble to prove his point. She had tried to tell him he was not the father as she wanted rid of him. Now she was going to have a meeting with him in the family court, which was what Lily had to arrange. She enjoyed arranging and sitting in on these cases, as this was furthering her career towards the position of a judge. If she gave up her job with the company she was working for, to shift, it would be a step back and she didn't want to miss this opportunity. But in the end, it had to come down to what was best for them all as a family.

Kennedy was at the cemetery today to put flowers on his mother's grave and was surprised to find someone had been before him and left a beautiful bouquet. He wondered who the unknown visitor was. The only person he could think would do this was Lily, so he rang her on his cell phone. "Hi Lily, have you been to the cemetery and left flowers on mother's grave?" He was surprised when she told him she hadn't had time to visit. This left him puzzled.

On further inspection he saw a note partly hidden by the flowers so he proceeded to read it. He was shocked! It read: 'Rest in peace, Mother'. He had a sudden thought: had the twins she abandoned learned of their mother's passing, and were these flowers left by them? If it was, Kennedy wished he could have made contact with them, as he hoped to do this one day. For the time being it would remain a mystery!

Cryptocurrency makes headlines

The big talk at Kennedy's workplace this week was about bitcoin. His superiors were holding a meeting, as there was a lot of negative publicity about cryptocurrency once again. This was not going to help it keep its value if this persisted! The top man, who had his finger on the pulse, pointed out it was just a correction in the world market. In the United States inflation had jumped more than expected in June and bitcoin and Ethereum's fluctuation reached forty-year highs. He pointed out that crypto asset prices weren't correlated with the global economy as much as stock markets. Because the country was in a highly volatile environment, it was almost impossible to predict the future with any degree of certainty. But regardless of when the economic growth returned, it was predicted that bitcoin would still be a better bet than most other assets. It would remain intact and continue the process of becoming the benchmark digital collateral in a world going that way. Crypto is not just a volatile market; it is an unpredictable one, and this is one of its strengths. It is filled with talented, ambitious and driven people who will continue to come up with new technologies and innovative ways to deal with the old ones.

Kennedy was always in on these briefings as he hoped to be able to persuade his partners what was going to be a good investment. As with NFTs, the market was experiencing a correction or adjustment. Beeple's artwork created a digital gold rush, attracting both Wall Street and Main Street investors into its space, in an attempt to become overnight billionaires. Many did, but others lost out! This proved the NFTs market was far from over as it was still generating billions of dollars in sales volume. As Kennedy and his partners had experienced, blue-chip collections were among the most traded despite the plunge in numbers, but this was due to a consolidation period.

After picking up on this information, he was wondering if he had put Lincoln and Reece wrong with deciding to go with a new digital artist. Perhaps they should have stuck with their original one, the blue-chip artist. Only time would tell. But one spark of hope was that the NFTs' value decreased at a lower rate than underlying cryptocurrencies during the down months. Because of its capacity to reduce fraud in the art world, it was generally thought NFTs were here to stay.

Reece was still working late at nights, so this left the gate wide open for Kennedy to spend more time with

Mackenzie, Harrison and Leila. They loved it when he visited as he was a fun person to be around, and this made for a happy household. It didn't seem to worry Reece that he spent so much time at their home, but of course he was a good loyal friend!

It wasn't only the kids that looked forward to his visits, as Lily was just as happy. Reece seemed so caught up in his work lately, trying to get everything organised for when he started his new position in Auckland. Lily was still very much against the shift. The only person it really suited was Reece as everyone else was happy to stay in their present environment. She had asked Leila if she wanted to move to a new home in another town and her response was, "What about Uncle Kennedy? Is he coming with us?" When she learnt he wasn't, she didn't want to move. Besides, she had made friends at play group. Lily knew the time was drawing near when they would have to sit down and make a final decision.

Kennedy had been to the market to buy a bunch of flowers to take to the cemetery today. He often thought about his mother's wretched life and it left him in tears, but then he had to remind himself she abandoned her children, so she was her own worst enemy. Her life could have been so different if she had faced her responsibilities.

As he pulled up at the entrance to the cemetery carpark, he was surprised to see Lily's car parked there. Just the thought of catching up with her sent his head into a tailspin. As he walked towards his mother's grave, he was surprised to see Reece kneeling in front of her headstone. He stopped and observed, then noticed the fresh flowers that were lying there. Was it Reece who had been leaving flowers? But why? Then a flash of discomfort engulfed him. Surely the flowers from last week couldn't have been his, as he remembered what was written on the note, 'Rest in peace, Mother'. No, that did not make any sense, she was his mother, not Reece's.

Kennedy didn't know whether to turn and go but whatever he decided, it was too late as Reece had seen him. They had surprised each other so this made for an awkward meeting. It was Reece who spoke first as he came towards Kennedy. "I have just left some flowers by Mother's headstone."

This completely threw Kennedy. What did he mean 'Mother's headstone'? "What are you talking about, Reece? Your parents have passed away. Did you leave flowers here last week?"

It was now time for Reece to tell Kennedy about his adoption. "I only found out after my parents died that I was adopted. Your mother was telling the truth all along. I was the baby she put up for adoption. Do you realise that makes us half-brothers?"

Kennedy went down on his knees. The first thought that came to his mind was he had cheated on his own brother. To have cheated on his best friend was bad enough, but his own brother, this brought tears as he was a guy with deep feelings.

Where did this leave him? Reece was surprised by Kennedy's behaviour. Why was this so upsetting? He thought this news would make him happy. "What is wrong?" he asked.

Kennedy was lost for words, and he could barely bring himself to look at Reece. How could he explain his shock? It took a few minutes for him to gather his words, "I'm sorry, it's just that all the time I thought Mother was delusional when she was telling the truth. I am just coming to terms with the fact we are half-brothers. Our lives have been so different and to think it took a stranger to come into our lives. If she had not contacted me, we would never have known, and it would have remained a secret to the end. But why didn't you tell us you were adopted?"

Reece told him he was still coming to terms with it, and it was too hard for him to tell anyone. "It wasn't until Mother turned up and then everything fell into place. She knew the minute she saw me that I was Peter's and her son. Now I know why I didn't inherit my mother's and father's intelligence. My biological father worked behind the counter in a department store – hardly the background for an intelligent mind. I can put that theory to bed and get on with life! It was interesting for me to find out that twins were in my genes, hence the birth of Mackenzie and Harrison, my very own twins. This statement nearly cut Kennedy in half; they were his twins not Reece's. He felt at this moment his world was starting to disintegrate. Guilt, deceit and untold truths were secrets he had to try to hide from his own brother.

The next meeting between Lily and Kennedy was not as romantic as Lily had planned. She wondered why he had not been to visit the children. She had had terrible trouble trying to contact him, which was most unusual. "Why haven't you been to see us?" she asked.

He sat down and put his hands up to his head trying to cradle it, then the tears started; where was he going to start? He was still devastated with all the information that was swirling in his head. "Did Reece tell you we are half-brothers; we both shared the same mother?"

Lily had to think quickly before she spoke, as she had known this since the DNA tests that they were related. "No, he hasn't spoken to me about that. When did he tell you?"

Kennedy explained what had transpired at the cemetery between them both. "That is the reason I haven't been to visit, Lily; I don't know what to do. I have betrayed my own brother. When mother mentioned the children were cousins. I didn't understand what she was saying, but now it all rings true. Of course, the only person that doesn't know this is Reece. My love for you will never change. I am no good as a lover to anyone else. I have never forgiven myself for what I did to you and still carry that remorse every day. For you to have given me the twins is more than I could have wished for, but where do we go from here?"

"What do you mean?" asked Lily.

Kennedy was totally lost in his own mind, and all he could think of was the word 'betrayal'. He had betrayed his own brother, the very person who had put his inheritance into making the wealth the three of them shared today. "Tell me what you think we should do, Lily?"

She could not imagine her life without Kennedy's

visits and the children would miss him. "Please don't desert us, your guilt is my guilt, and this is something we will have to carry together. Can we just carry on as usual? I know things have changed in the outside world, but our world doesn't have to change. We are lovers and we are parents to two babies who you love dearly. Don't let us fall apart because of what has happened," she pleaded. Lily could see he was upset so she went over and put her arms around him. He responded, crushing her tightly to his chest.

"Give me time to think this over, my darling. I'm trying to come to terms with everything, but it has overwhelmed me."

Lily knew this was going to take time as Kennedy was always absorbed in his feelings.

The time had come for Reece to pin down Lily and discuss their up-and-coming shift, as so far their conversations had led to nothing. Lily always brought the discussion to an end before they could reach a compromise. But that was not going to happen tonight as Reece was determined. They would talk until there was some sort of agreement. It was starting to affect their marriage as the subject was always put on hold.

"Right, Lily, where do you stand with our shift? I want an answer from you now, as I have only two weeks before I start my new management position. We have to make some plans," he told her.

Lily was going to find it hard to tell Reece how she felt as she knew he would be upset. "I'm sorry, Reece, I don't want to uproot the family and I have my job to consider.

How would you feel about commuting for a couple of months until we see how that works?" she asked.

"But I want to see my children, Lily. That's no good to me."

She told him that lately he hadn't had much to do with them as he was too preoccupied with his work. "I can't just walk out on my job as I have personal clients to look after. Please can we give it a go?" she pleaded.

What could Reece say? He sensed all along that she didn't want to shift, but he held on to hope she might change her mind. That was not going to happen! "Okay, Lily, I will give it a go for two months, but if I miss you and the children, then I expect you to come to Auckland."

Lily would not let it rest there, so she told him they would review it nearer the time. He was not happy but decided to leave it as it would end up in another argument. This new promotion was important to him as he felt it would make people take more notice. He wanted more than ever to prove that his newly found background wasn't a deterrent to him getting on. It wasn't about the money, it was about his self-worth, as this had always been an issue for him. He still felt he was not as smart as Kennedy and Lincoln.

Tonight was the last meeting the lads would have before Reece left for Auckland, so there were decisions to be made. First on the agenda was to see how their cryptocurrency wallet was holding up. Sadly the bitcoin had let them down again, but there had been talk of a correction so hopefully this was the reason. The bidding date on their NFT digital art piece had expired yesterday so now it was time to see if Kennedy's decision was the right one. He chose to switch from their blue-chip digital creator to a new artist. This new art was 'crypto-punk' and the first piece in the series had sold for $11.5 million, so he had high hopes this one would do well. So into their NFT wallet they went and were pleasantly surprised as the final bid was for $7.5 million. The switch had paid off handsomely.

It was now decision time: were they going to carry on with their investments or would they divide their net worth into three equal shares? Reece had already put some thought into it and decided they should take equal shares. To bow out as multi-millionaires was a satisfying thought.

Kennedy was shocked to hear what Reece was suggesting as he thought they were a formidable team. "What made you think of us splitting up?" he asked. "We want you to stay in our investment portfolio, Reece."

"I don't think I contribute enough, and my understanding of NFTs is limited. I can't seem to get my head around the way it works."

"But you don't have to worry; we can look after it for you. Remember one thing, Reece. If it wasn't for your backing, neither Lincoln nor I would be in the position we are today. You have made us into millionaires, so please give it some thought, but we would like you to still be part of our investment portfolio," said Kennedy.

Reece said he would think about it as he had so many things going on in his head. The ongoing saga of his biological mother and then to find out his best friend was his half-brother had left him in a quandary. His life was not as he thought it to be.

Lily and Kennedy's relationship had entered a cooling-off period, as knowing he was cheating on his half-brother had affected Kennedy. Lily knew it would hurt him deep down as his feelings played a big part in his life, which is what she loved about him. He wasn't afraid to express how he felt, and she remembered their quiz days when she thought he was a pompous and arrogant young man. Sometimes little snippets came back of the night when he took her without consent, but she had forgiven him. He didn't hurt her and now she realised it was out of love not malice, as he kept apologising and declaring his love for her. He spent time with the children but did not hang around, as guilt plagued him. He missed his special moments with Lily and didn't know how long it would take before they could resume their affair. She missed him but understood why.

The divided family

Today there were final farewells as Reece gathered the last of his belongings. Last night's party was a reminder of the friendship between the three young lads, whose fortunes had grown far beyond their wildest dreams. Reece was going to be missed and he had finally made up his mind to stay in their crypto investment, knowing it was in good hands.

Lily and the children gave Reece kisses as he climbed into his vehicle, then waved goodbye. He was driving to Picton, then crossing on the ferry and driving on to Auckland. He wanted to leave his vehicle there so he could be independent and would fly home to visit the family.

He knew he had a challenge ahead of him as he had no say in employing the present staff; that was done by the CEO of the company. For the first few days he walked around and got to know the staff and what departments they worked in. His assistant manager, Natalia, seemed an astute young lady who had an advantage over him, as she had worked alongside the staff. Reece decided to work out in his own mind whether he was satisfied with their work ethics, as he was told the staffing was now his business, and he could hire and fire.

A week had passed and Reece could see some room for improvement in certain areas, so he called a staff meeting. He pointed out where he wanted things to change, so now they knew what was expected of them. This did not go down well with the assistant manager, so she made her opinion known to Reece. He could see she had a strong personality, so he let her know that if he needed her advice, he would ask for it. This caused an instant stand-off between them. He had encountered this before and knew from experience that the boss had to be just that, or there would end up being two managers running the hotel. This would not be happening!

As the general manager he had a suite in the hotel so he could be on call if needed. The staff all knew how to get hold of him in an emergency. The hotel had 110 rooms and catered mainly for commercial travellers and business people. It had a large conference room that proved to be very popular, attracting many conferences. Because Reece wasn't familiar with this side of the business, he held a meeting with Natalia to allow her to bring him up to date in this field. She came into his office with her guard up, but that soon disappeared when she knew he had to depend upon her knowledge in certain areas. This was their first official meeting together and he was feeling a bit more at ease, as he saw a softer side to her. He knew first introductions could be awkward until a boundary was formed, so wrong opinions could be formed. After this meeting he felt perhaps they could work together without any hostility.

A fortnight had passed, and Lily and Kennedy had resumed their friendship. Now that Reece was out of sight Kennedy had no reminders of the word 'betrayal'. Each night after work he came around to help Lily with the children, and he would play with them while she cooked dinner. The twins were walking around the furniture holding on for dear life, in case they lost their balance. They hadn't quite worked out yet that they could walk without help.

After dinner they were showered and put to bed, then Kennedy was called upon to read stories. This was all new to the family, as Reece never had time to read to them; he had not been a hands-on dad. Lily was left to handle everything when she arrived home from work, so to have Kennedy's help was a godsend. The nanny handled all the daytime chores along with the children until Lily arrived home.

Once the children were settled, Lily and Kennedy would sit down to a coffee and talk over their day's work. Kennedy would not make love to Lily in Reece's home. Their love sessions were strictly at Kennedy's place. At times it was hard not to whip Lily into the bedroom and take her, but he knew the guilt would be too much. Lily had wanted this to happen several times as love welled through her body and the moment was right, but Kennedy kept to his word. It was hard at times to say no, as his body ached for her, but he had made rules he would abide by.

Lily wondered where the time had gone, as it was nearly three weeks that Reece had been away. He called them twice a week to speak with her and the children and she thought he seemed preoccupied with his work sometimes when they spoke. There had been no mention of her shifting, which was a welcome relief. He told her he was finding it challenging but loved everything about his promotion. She suspected this was because he was still trying to prove himself to the world.

Lily was surprised that she hadn't really missed Reece as much as she thought she would, but of course Kennedy was filling that role. She would ring Kennedy at his work and let him know she was waiting for him all showered up and in his bed keeping it warm for him. This was all the encouragement he needed and within fifteen minutes he would pull up in the driveway and make a mad dash inside, to find Lily ready for him. The touching would begin, his hands roamed all over her body, gently caressing her as she lay there loving every minute. This was Kennedy's trademark, he felt he had to earn his big moment, so worked her body until she begged to be taken. Then she would pull him close to her and guide his manly parts to her waiting body. He was the ultimate lover, always expressing his feelings for her. She hadn't experienced such tenderness until they became lovers. She knew now she could never live without him and if it had to come to a choice, she knew where her heart lay.

In the District Court today, Lily had stood with her client as his defence lawyer, as they were going for the joint custody of his estranged daughter. It had taken over one year to advance to this stage, as the court system was overwhelmed with cases waiting to be heard. The ex-partner had made it difficult for her client, as she was upset that he had proved by DNA that he was her biological father. She had hoped he never knew about his daughter as they had parted seven years ago and now she was in a new relationship.

Lily loved the court scene; it was her ultimate dream, and every case she represented in court was a step nearer reaching her goal. Deep down she hoped she was never going to be in this position, but it wasn't beyond happening. The judge listened to both sides of their stories and tried to remain impartial, but she pointed out that the ex-partner had tried to conceal the fact that Lily's client was the biological father and therefore was entitled to parental rights. An outburst followed, "But he has had nothing to do with bringing up my daughter!" she yelled.

"Of course he hasn't, because you never gave him the opportunity, and please address me as 'Your Honour'," chided the judge. This reprimand certainly put the woman in her place. After deliberation, the judge ruled that Lily's client was entitled to have his daughter for two nights a week. This was to be discussed amicably between both parties.

As Lily left the court her client asked her to have lunch

with him, which she accepted because she was hungry, so they popped into a nearby café. It was here he told Lily he would like to further their acquaintance. This came somewhat as a surprise, but she knew it was not good practice to indulge in a friendship with a client; in the legal profession it was not seen to be proper.

Lily told him she was married with children. He accepted this then asked her what her qualifications were. She told him she had her Bachelor of Laws and had completed her Professional Legal Study so this left her with several more years in the legal profession before she was able to apply for a position as a Judge. She hoped one day to be in partnership in a law firm, as this would stand her in good stead. But first she had to become a District Court Judge which handled family and youth issues. Next came the position of High Court Judge which handled serious criminal and civil cases with the disputed amount being $350 or more. She told her client she fully intended to get to the High Court. Then came the Court of Appeal and the Supreme Court, but she felt these were out of her reach. "If you set your goals high enough you will get there," he told her. What a pity she was taken, he thought to himself, as he enjoyed her company. He would certainly put in a good word for her at her workplace.

It seemed strange not to have Reece at their meeting, but Lincoln and Kennedy knew what to do, as they were working in the right places to know what was in hot demand. Several of Kennedy's workmates in the financial sector also delved into the crypto world so there were plenty of ideas floating around. Bitcoin had lost its place to NFTs as these were the fashionable investment of the moment. Investors were becoming millionaires overnight as the ones that could afford to follow the blue-chip digital creators were the ones coming out on top. Kennedy was not keen on spending $5 to 7 million on one artwork, so he was studying the newbies, the up-and-coming artists, as he had to be mindful he was playing with Lincoln's and Reece's livelihoods, not just his own.

They both studied the new creators and decided to stick with the 'crypto-punk' series, as it had been good to them and could still be bought for a realistic price. Not that they could buy it for their previous price as it had doubled in a period of three weeks. They would pay the asking price of $1 million and hope that when they put it back on the NFTs trading platform of OpenSea, the largest NFT marketplace, it would double in price again. The creators loved to see their art selling multiple times as they received royalties on each sale. This was why artists and creators used the NFTs platform to sell their digital artworks, as there was no greedy middleman with his fingers in the pie, or art galleries taking their spoils. It was a market where the buyer decides on the price they are prepared to pay, then hopes to move it on for a handsome profit … this is called speculation!

Now it was down to choosing an artwork and deciding on a price at which to buy. The one they chose was the fourth in a series of 'crypto-punk', so out of their NFT wallet came $1 million to secure their new purchase. This was a direct sale so as soon as the money was received by the seller, it belonged to them. The person who owned it before them had probably doubled their money by being the first purchaser. All they had to do now was wait for a week and then put it up for auction and hope it sold for a healthy price. Kennedy remembered reading a quote from a popular creator that read, 'If everyone wants it, then it has a value'. Lincoln thought this was an appropriate saying when referring to the digital art world.

Lincoln had wanted to ask Kennedy ever since he knew they were half-brothers' what impact it had had on his life. Had it changed things in any way? The right moment had come, so now was the time. "Tell me, Kennedy, are your feelings different after going from friends to being family, between you and Reece?"

Kennedy wasn't expecting this and was surprised by his own admission. "When someone enters your life who you knew had walked out on you, your life is turned upside down, leaving you in limbo. I think it was easier for Reece and me to be friends than half-brothers. I'm still coming to terms with some personal issues, but this is my problem," he confessed.

Lincoln had not been blind to the fact that Kennedy was in love with Lily and that was why he had given up on dating other girls. "I have known all along that you fancied Lily, but I kept it to myself. All I ask is that you do not cause a family breakup as Reece loves his three children."

Kennedy couldn't hold it any longer, being the emotional guy he was. "The twins are Lily's and mine. Leila is Reece's daughter," he declared.

"What do you mean?" asked a shocked Lincoln.

Now it was time for Kennedy to tell him what had happened and why it happened.

"Good God man, you certainly have got personal issues. What the hell are you going to do? To cheat on a good friend is bad enough but to cheat on your half-brother is the pits," added Lincoln.

"I know, that's what I am finding hard to come to terms with. I don't know what to do," Kennedy replied.

Lincoln took his time and thought on this scenario, then he came up with the only sensible solution. "Our three-way partnership must end. We will hold a meeting with Reece and divide our investments into three equal shares and go our separate ways. It doesn't necessarily mean the end of our friendships, but it will make it easier for you, Kennedy. Is the affair still ongoing?" he asked.

Kennedy told him he loved Lily, always had and always would, and he couldn't love anyone else. "Where is this going to end up, where does Reece fit into the picture?" Lincoln asked, as he could see his friend was heartbroken.

"That's why it is so hard for me, as he was the one that trusted us, and I have let him down. He shared his wealth with us, making us into millionaires. Please help me, Lincoln. I can't give Lily up. I am so lost."

There was silence as the two men stood looking at each other. It was Lincoln who spoke first. "The investment partnership could not have happened just by one person with the finance. Reece needed the two of us and our knowledge to break into the crypto world. We have all contributed equally and benefitted handsomely.

Don't feel guilty about the money issue, but the personal front is a different matter. Rather you than me! Your secret is safe with me my friend, but tread carefully! When Reece comes home, we will talk and all agree to dissolve our investments and go our separate ways. If the crypto world collapses, we at least have our money, although I will carry on dabbling. I love the challenge."

It was Monday morning and Lily and the children were at the airport waiting for Reece's plane to land. It was a month since they had seen him and they were excited, all apart from Lily as she didn't know how she would feel, and perhaps only time would tell. As he came through the terminal Leila saw him first and ran straight up to him. "Daddy, Daddy, you're back," she cried in excitement. Reece lifted her up and cuddled her then walked over to Lily and the twins. "Hi ratbags," he greeted the twins, then gave Lily a hug. "It's lovely to be home again with my family."

Kennedy told Lily he would stay away for the first couple of days so they could be together as a family. Reece would probably like her to himself. Although it hurt, this was just the way it had to be, just now. Lily opened a bottle of wine to celebrate, so they sat on the settee, with the kids climbing all over them. Five minutes later Reece asked Leila to play with the twins so they could have a drink in peace.

Reece told Lily all about the hotel and his staff and how he loved his position as general manager. He had a nice suite in the hotel, and everything was working out great. "Mummy, we are hungry," Leila reminded her.

"You get dinner and I will call the hotel and see that all is okay," Reece told Lily. She was a little upset, as he hadn't even asked how she had managed on her own or mentioned her work.

After dinner Reece relaxed while Lily bathed the children and read them their bedtime stories. This was when she missed Kennedy as he shared all these duties with her, which made it fun, not a household chore. As the night drew to a close, Reece suggested they go to bed. Lily went and had a shower and by the time she went back to the bedroom, Reece was tucked up sound asleep. She had thought perhaps he might want to make love, but obviously not. In a way she wasn't unhappy, as since his return she hadn't felt any spark between them. Was this the end of their marriage or was she expecting too much? She decided to leave the verdict open and hope things felt different tomorrow.

At some ungodly hour Lily was woken by Reece's phone. He was still asleep, so she answered it. "Hi Reece, it's Natalia. The conference has just finished; it all went well. I'm just going to fall into your bed, as it's too late to go home. How is everything at your home?"

Lily didn't know what to say so she pushed the 'end' button and put the phone back. Who was Natalia, and why was she sleeping in his bed? Is this why Reece didn't want her tonight? Did he have a new bedmate?

Reece woke before Lily so dressed and went to the kitchen and made himself a coffee. The children were starting to wander around so he told them to wake their mother.

"Mummy, time to get up," said Leila. As soon as Lily saw the time she jumped out of bed as she had a meeting at work at 8.30am. She dressed and then got the kids some breakfast. Where was Reece? She looked out the window and he was sitting on the porch talking on his phone. The nanny had just arrived, so Lily left her to see to the children. She called out to Reece to say she was away to work, and he gave her a wave and kept talking. This was not the morning greeting Lily expected. She hoped at least there would be a kiss before she left for work, but this apparently was not to be!

She was interested to find out what was in store at their work meeting this morning, as they all had to assemble in the boardroom. Once seated, the CEO of the law office announced he was leaving for a position overseas, so his share of the company was going to sold. "I would like to think one of our legal team would be interested in buying my share, so it doesn't fall into the hands of our opposition. It would be satisfying to see it stay within our own office."

Lily felt this was her big break. She knew Reece had money invested in cryptocurrency so perhaps he would help her buy the share up for sale. She knew this was a requirement to advance to the High Court Judge position she so desired. Tonight, she would talk with him and get his opinion. Lily could see no stumbling block in the way, as it was the largest legal office in the city, well known and well-staffed. If it all came off, it would be her dream come true. She was excited.

Lily arrived home in a jubilant mood, imagining

herself as part owner of their legal office. The nanny had organised tea for the children, so she decided to cook a nice meal for Reece and herself. Once the children had eaten, she showered them and put them into their pyjamas, so they were ready to pop into bed at their usual time. She heard Reece talking on his cell phone so went ahead and prepared a nice meal for them to have together, as this would give them time to talk.

Just before she was about to serve, the nanny appeared in the kitchen. "What are you doing back?" she asked in a surprised voice. "Hasn't Reece told you? He is taking you out for dinner. I am babysitting." This knocked Lily for six, as Reece hadn't said anything. Mind you, he was still on his phone.

"Go and change into your glad-rags," the nanny whispered to her. Lily went to their bedroom and sat on the bed. She felt disappointed as she had her night all planned. Now when was she going to get the chance to talk with Reece?

"Hurry up, Lily, we are leaving soon," announced Reece as he entered the bedroom.

"Where are we going?" she asked.

"I have arranged a dinner with Lincoln and Megan and Kennedy, and we lads are having a meeting back at Lincoln's pad after we have eaten."

The only encouraging thought was the fact she would see Kennedy. She had missed him in so many ways: his hands-on care with the children and especially his hands-on care with her. Lily had noticed since Reece's return that he wasn't much interested in the family side of life.

Was this because he was used to the peace and quiet of his suite with no interruptions? But surely he missed the children.

Everyone was seated at their favourite restaurant, Lugano's, where Reece was the topic of conversation. He was very proud of his new position as general manager, and it made him feel important, so he let them all know. Lily realised in that moment that he had changed, and his focus was very much centred on himself. Had his new position gone to his head? Then she remembered the early-morning phone call from Natalia; she hadn't even had time to discuss this with him. She felt it wasn't important any more. Last night it had been a shock, but as tonight progressed the less important it became. Lily stole glances at Kennedy, and this lifted her mood. This did not go unnoticed by Lincoln.

After they finished dinner they drove around to Lincoln's pad, where the boys retreated to his computer room, while the girls opened a bottle of wine and settled in to share girls' talk. This was the meeting where Lincoln and Kennedy were going to tell Reece they had talked about dividing their investments and going their separate ways. But first they had to make a decision on their latest art purchase, as it was now time to put it up for auction. They decided on the OpenSea platform with a two-week bidding period. They hoped to capitalise big time on their 'crypto-punk artwork.

Now it was down to business. Lincoln started: "Reece, last time we talked about buying our latest NFTs artwork, you said you wanted out, but we talked you into staying in. I think the time has come for us to divide our fortune into three equal shares to allow each of us to flourish in our chosen fields. How do you feel about this?" he asked.

Reece thought for a moment. It was his dream one day to own his own hotel, so perhaps now was the time for him to consider his wealth. If he left it in cryptocurrencies and the market crashed, his dream would be shattered, so, yes, now was the time.

"Yes, guys, I think that is a great idea, as I have future plans," he told them.

They agreed to wait until their last digital artwork had sold then they would divide their wealth. He asked Kennedy what he was going to do with his share. "I have no idea at the moment, but I will try to find ways to dodge any taxes we have to pay, so leave this part up to me." Lincoln told them he was still going to dabble in the crypto world, as he liked the challenge and the unknown. If his fortune dipped, it wouldn't affect him too much as he had no commitments and a well-paying job, so he would just cruise along and ride the wave.

They did a rough calculation on how much a third of their wealth was worth. The bitcoin currency had come down substantially from its highest peak. At the very start they had paid $150 per bitcoin, then it skyrocketed to $69,000 per coin, and then dipped to its current price of $39,000. It had made them a profit of $195 million for their investment of $5 million. This did not include their NFTs wallet as they would finalise this when their last sale went through. So their net worth each was roughly $70 million, providing nothing drastic happened to the crypto market before they sold out. Next would be the transfer fees and taxes, but Kennedy was working on that. He knew that in Germany, Switzerland, Singapore, Denmark and Puerto Rico (a crypto haven) that bitcoin was not subject to taxes, but that would soon change. In America cryptocurrency was unfortunately recognised as 'property' and therefore subject to a capital gains tax. The US government had invested in specialist software to track bitcoin transactions and other cryptocurrencies.

Cryptocurrency is relatively new in the investment world, so the bottom line is that it is an exciting space with lots of opportunities, and governments were just beginning to come to terms with how to tax these investors. Kennedy was not sure of New Zealand's policy, but he would look into it. He had been more interested in overseas policies until now, but this was his country so he would have to follow up on it. What he found amusing was the fact that governments didn't recognise cryptocurrency as legal tender, but their tax agencies wanted some of the profits in taxes.

The lads had achieved a lot tonight, so they decided to meet next time Reece flew home and finalise their three-way split. It was now time to join the girls, so the tops came off another couple of bottles of wine. Lincoln sat and watched the situation unfolding before him, although he had had a couple of wines and his brain was a little foggy, the vibes that were passing between Kennedy and Lily did not escape him. He felt sad that Kennedy had fallen in love with someone who belonged to another. He was the playboy of their group who had dated some of the most glamourous girls, but still love eluded him. He was waiting to find the one that he thought matched his intelligence, then Lily appeared. At first, Kennedy had been jealous of her knowledge and by the time his feelings for her kicked in, Reece had nabbed her.

When Lincoln learnt from Kennedy how this affair all started, he was disappointed in him. Kennedy told Lincoln that he had taken Lily against her will, and in his eyes this was rape, but when he listened to Kennedy's story, his thinking changed. Lincoln felt sad as Kennedy had turned into the most caring person, and he could see Lily was the love of his life.

Lincoln had noticed a change in Reece recently. He seemed to be continuing to have to prove himself in the business world. And he hadn't realised that brains weren't the be-all and end-all of their success; it was really his inheritance that had played the biggest part in all of this, as without it they would not be as well off as they were today. Lincoln could see heartache down the track, but he didn't know for whom!

Drifting apart

By the time Reece and Lily arrived home it was very late, the nanny had gone to bed in the guest bedroom and when Lily peeped in on her she was sound asleep, so she quietly closed the door. It was now time to talk to Reece, but all he wanted to do was fall into bed. She didn't argue as she thought they would talk while lying close to each other. As she undressed, she noticed Reece staring at her and she felt a little embarrassed, so jumped quickly into bed. Reece climbed in and moved close to her, then she felt his hands clutching her buttocks and pulling her hard against him and before she realised, he had entered her.

Lily was shocked. Where were the feelings that should have passed between them before this happened? Instead, she felt used, not loved! Then it was all over, and Reece turned his back and dropped off to sleep. It was not a night she would remember; in fact, it was one she would rather forget. She felt so disappointed with Reece's insensitive lovemaking, and tears came to her eyes so she turned her back and cried silently.

As much as she tried to rekindle her love for him, there was nothing there. She felt so alone lying next to him; he was just a stranger in her bed. Lily had tried not to bring Kennedy in on her family time with Reece, but right now she wished it was him in her bed. But for the children, she had to try to make things work between herself and Reece so they remained a family.

When Lily woke Reece was not in their bed. She had taken the day off work to spend time with him before he caught his flight back to Auckland at 3 o'clock. The house was quiet which was unusual at this time in the mornings, but of course, the nanny would be up and attending to the children. She showered then dressed and walked into dining room to find everyone at the breakfast table, everyone except Reece.

"Have you seen Reece?" Lily asked the nanny.

"He's on the back patio talking on his cell phone."

"I want to have a talk with him before he flies out. Could you please tend to the children?"

The nanny agreed so she went out to join Reece on the patio. He was still on his phone so she sat beside him. He hurriedly ended the call with "Bye Natalia, I'll see you later today." Was this Lily's chance to ask who Natalia was? No, she wouldn't worry as she was totally over it.

"Reece, I want to talk to you about buying a share in our legal firm. One of our CEOs is shifting overseas so his share can be bought. It would help me in my quest towards becoming a High Court Judge, if I was a shareholder in a law firm."

Reece looked at Lily. She was his children's mother, so, no, he did not like that idea at all. "I'm sorry, Lily. One day I will own my own hotel and you and the children will have to come and live with me."

This was not what Lily expected to hear. "But, Reece, you knew I wanted to pursue a career in law; it has always been my dream."

"No, Lily, your place is with us as a family," he replied in an adamant voice.

This left Lily disappointed once again, so she asked Reece to reconsider.

"I won't change my mind; this is the way it has got to be," was his final answer.

She sat there and looked at Reece. What was happening to him? He wasn't the same guy she fell in love with. Their silence was broken by Leila as she came bounding towards them. "Daddy, come and listen to me read," she said.

With this he got up and followed her inside. Lily stayed sitting on the patio with her head in her hands and wept silently. This was not the outcome she wanted to hear, as she could see her future slipping away. Was her dream beyond her reach?

As they were driving to the airport, it was just Lily and Reece in the car. She decided to have one last go at speaking with him. "Reece, will you please think about what I have asked you? It is important to me."

"I'm sorry, Lily, but your place is with me and our

family. When I buy my own hotel, I want you to be part of it."

Hurt filled her belly. She was happy they were parting, otherwise she might have said something she would have been sorry for. Lily dropped Reece off at the front entrance of the airport as she didn't want to see him off; her feelings were overwhelming sad. He came around and kissed her goodbye then he was gone. It was only then she realised he had not even mentioned the fact that he had originally asked her and the family to come and live with him in Auckland. Tears trickled down her cheeks as she drove home, and she felt upset and hurt – not about not being asked to move, but because of his refusal to help her with the purchase of part of the law practice.

As she entered her home, the nanny was about to leave so she had to pick herself up and become a mother to the children. She prepared them tea and they sat around the table chatting. "Is Daddy going to be away for a long time?" asked Leila. Lily assured her he would be back soon.

"I'm glad Uncle Kennedy is still here; he plays with us and makes us laugh."

Had she noticed that her father hadn't spent much time with them, she wondered? Suddenly the doorbell rang and Leila ran to answer it. "Uncle Kennedy is here," she announced, and that was enough for the twins to make a beeline for the door. In he came with three little ones in his arms. Just the sight of the love that he showered on the children sent Lily to her bedroom in tears.

"What's wrong with Mummy?" asked Leila. Kennedy told her he would go and see, so made his way to her bedroom, where he found her lying on the bed crying. He went and sat beside her and stroked her shoulders. "What is wrong, my darling?" he asked.

Lily couldn't answer but he could see she was in quite a state, so told her to rest and he would be there if she needed him. Just the mention of the word 'needed' was all she wanted to hear. "Please sit with me and hold me," she asked him. He knew then that something had happened between her and Reece. He wouldn't ask about it, as she would tell him when she was ready. "I'll put the children to bed and read to them. You rest, and we will talk later," he told her.

"Come, Leila, I'll get you and the twins ready for bed. Mummy's tired so we will let her rest." He was capable of caring for the kids. He loved them and was so proud. Mackenzie and Harrison were nearly two years old, so they were into everything, especially Harrison, who was a typical boy. Mackenzie was the spitting image of her mother and for this Kennedy was ecstatic, as he had the love of his life and a mini love. Although Leila was Reece's daughter, she was a bright child and had inherited her mother's brains. Now that the truth had come out about Reece's background, Kennedy understood why he was the way he was. He was still coming to terms with the fact that he and Reece shared the same mother. In fact, it had impacted on their friendship, especially now that he knew he was in love with his half-brother's wife! Kennedy convinced himself he had no control over who he fell in love with as his heart ruled his head. If he hadn't been such a playboy then he might have realised sooner that he had feelings for Lily, but Reece got in first, and by then it was all too late.

The children were all tucked in bed and read to, so silence reigned. Kennedy went back to Lily's bedroom to see if she was okay and was surprised to find her sound asleep. She was still fully dressed so he pulled up the bedspread and covered her, then he lay beside her. This was one rule he had made; he would not make love to Lily in Reece's bed. This was the matrimonial bed and he would not break this promise he had made to himself. He lay there with his arms around her, and just to be this near to her sent warm vibes through his body.

As he lay there, he wondered what had upset Lily. He didn't have to wait long as she stirred and sat up in fright; where was she? Then it all came flooding back, and that feeling of disappointment was still there. She felt used as she recalled Reece's cold attempt at lovemaking!

"I will make us a cup of coffee, so come out to the lounge when you are ready. I'll be waiting," he told her. He did not feel comfortable even just lying on Reece's bed, as he felt he was crossing a dangerous line. He got up and went and put the kettle on.

When Lily came out, she had combed her hair and put a bit of makeup on, just to make herself look presentable. She liked to look nice for Kennedy as he was particular in his own appearance.

"How are you feeling now?" he asked.

Lily said she was coming right, but he could see she

was still troubled. "I know it's none of my business, Lily, but if you want to talk to me just go ahead."

She didn't know where to start as she had so much bottled up inside. "I asked Reece to help me out with some finance to buy into our law firm, as one of the CEOs is moving overseas so his share is up for grabs, but he refused. He wouldn't even consider it, even when I asked him to think about it. He told me he was going to buy a hotel and he wanted me to help him run it. I'm not interested in that sort of life. He knew right from the start I wanted to further my career in law and now he is not prepared to help me. It would help me move further up the ladder if I owned a share in a law practice, but it looks like I'm beat," she sighed in disappointment.

Kennedy listened and was angry that Reece wouldn't help her with some finance as he would have a small fortune when they sold their crypto portfolio. "Did Reece tell you we are dissolving our partnership and splitting the profit three ways? He will be a very wealthy man. I can't believe he wouldn't help you, Lily."

She was surprised to learn they were splitting; Reece hadn't said anything to her.

"I will buy the share in the law firm in your name. You are the mother of my two children, and I would love to do that for you, Lily. In fact I feel it is my duty to give you the opportunity to further your career. I know how important it is to you."

Lily was flabbergasted. Fancy Kennedy offering to buy the share, but, no, she couldn't let him do this. "No, Kennedy, it is not your responsibility. I am Reece's wife and therefore I feel it is his responsibility. You are such a caring person, that's what I love most about you."

"Listen to me, Lily, I want you to have it. If you leave it too long someone else will buy into it. It is a great opportunity as it is a reputable firm. We will go together tomorrow to the bank and I will transfer the money over to you."

"But you don't know how much it is worth," replied Lily.

Kennedy told her he was worth a lot of money, and he had no one other than her and the twins to give his money to. "I love you, Lily. There will never be anyone else for me. I look upon you as my partner, the mother of my children, so, please, I want to do this for you," he pleaded.

Lily knew within herself that one day she would leave Reece to be with Kennedy. He was such a caring person. This was made even more clear after Reece's short visit, and his unforgiving attempt to bed her, not love her, just use her! There was no love shown in the short time he was home, and he spent more time on his cell phone talking to Natalia, whoever she was.

During Lily's lunch break, Kennedy and Lily went to the bank and transferred over the amount needed to buy the share in her law firm. She was so happy as this was another step closer to reaching her dream. The company was happy that the share remained within the firm. Now Lily's name would appear on the partnership plaque that graced the wall as one entered the law practice. She arranged with Kennedy for him to leave work an hour early today and she would do the same. They would meet at his home as she wanted to reward him for his kind gesture today. It meant so much to her, and her dream was back on track.

They both arrived at the same time so Lily challenged Kennedy to see who could get undressed and into bed first. Of course, Kennedy won, as he had fewer clothes to remove. He had the bedspread pulled back ready for Lily to jump in beside him. It seemed a lifetime away since they had laid there together, but now was the time for them to do some catch-up. The seducing would have to be given a miss, as there were more important needs to be attended to. Lily wanted Kennedy to take her; she needed to be loved, she wanted to feel his body pressed hard against her, for them to come together as one.

The need for this was of utmost urgency. Her self-esteem had taken a tumble as she remembered Reece's lame attempt to make love to her. She needed to be built up again, to feel wanted, not used! Kennedy did not disappoint. His words were touching and reached her soul. He was a gentle, loving guy who knew how to treat a lady.

Six weeks had passed, and Lily was on top of the world. She was busy at work and to see her name on the partnership plaque outside the office each morning when she arrived at work set the mood for each day. She hadn't mentioned this to Reece as she felt he didn't need to know. Today she had to pick him up at the airport and was a little apprehensive as to how this visit would pan out.

They had spoken on the phone twice a week, but the conversation always revolved around Reece and his work. The children did get a mention each time, but it was as if they were an afterthought. There was never any mention of Lily's work.

Tomorrow was the big meeting at Lincoln's pad for the dissolving of their crypto partnership. They had their final NFTs digital art for sale, so wondered what the bidding had reached at the auction. Lily only knew this through Kennedy as Reece still hadn't told her that they were parting company. Did he not want her to know or had he just forgotten to tell her? Time would tell.

As she was waiting for Reece to come through the passenger terminal she had to go to the loo, and on her way back she saw Kennedy's father struggling with a large suitcase. She went to his aid, but just as she reached him, he fell in a heap on the floor. Lily thought he had tripped, but as she bent down to speak to him, she knew immediately that he needed medical help. She called for someone to ring for an ambulance.

Suddenly an airport medic came to assist her, but it was too late – Kennedy's father had died. Lily cradled him in her arms. Here lay Mackenzie and Harrison's grandfather, and the tears started so the medic asked if she knew him.

"Yes, he is my children's grandfather," she answered.

"Do you know who we should contact to let them know?" the medic asked.

Lily told him she would call his son. By this time people were starting to gather, so the medic called for airport staff to move the people on while they stretchered the body to a private area. Lily asked to stay with him, then she called Kennedy.

"What time was your father due back today? You weren't here to meet him."

"No, his plane isn't due for another two hours," he replied. It was then she had to tell him what had happened and that she was with his father. He was upset as his father had just come back from visiting his daughter, Kennedy's sister, in Canada. He had been gone for three months. His heart was broken as he had not even had a chance to say goodbye. "I'll be there in ten minutes. Please stay with him, my darling," he asked Lily.

Suddenly her phone rang and it was Reece. Oh my God, she had forgotten about him. "Where are you, Lily, I'm waiting for you?" he said in an agitated voice. It was then she told him where she was and what had happened and that she was sitting with Kennedy's father until he arrived.

"What about me?" Reece asked.

This reply shocked Lily, and she told him where to find her and if he wanted to go home, he could get the car keys off her and drive himself. Where was his empathy? This was not the man she had married; what had happened to that guy she once loved?

When Reece found her, he heard the medic talking to Lily. "How will the children take their grandfather's death?"

"They will be upset, but they are young so they will forget in time," she answered. It was then she saw Reece standing there. He wondered what this conversation was all about, as Kennedy's father didn't have any grandchildren that he knew of.

"I didn't know Robert had any grandchildren," he said.

Lily had to think of a quick answer. "I'll explain later. Here are the keys – you go home. The nanny leaves at five o'clock so you will have to look after the children. If I'm not home, get them some tea. There is plenty of food in the fridge that just needs to be heated." She didn't think this was a big request under the sad circumstances.

"Really, Lily, your place is at home with me and the children. I shouldn't have to feed them?"

She was furious. Kennedy had just lost his father, and his response caused her to let fly: "Think of people other than yourself. Your half-brother has just lost his father. Grow up and take some of the responsibility for your children, Reece." With this she threw the keys to him and walked away.

It was not like Lily to lose her cool, but her buttons had been pushed to the max. She sat and held Kennedy's father's hand. It felt cold. How sad that he didn't get to tell his son about his Canadian holiday. It must have been too much for him, but as yet they didn't know what the cause of death was, but a doctor was on his way.

When Kennedy arrived, he burst into tears when he found Lily still holding his father's hand. How brave was that? He went to his father and bent down and hugged him. "Why wasn't I here to be with you? Your plane wasn't due for another two hours. I never thought of it being early. I'm so sorry, Dad," he sobbed.

Lily knew Kennedy would take this to heart as he loved his father, and he was his life support since his mother walked out on her family responsibilities, all those years ago. "Don't beat yourself up, my love, he knew you loved him. He would not have known what happened, as he fell to the floor and was pronounced dead straight away; he didn't suffer. Let us be thankful for that," she said as she tried to comfort him.

It was then an announcement was made for someone to pick up the suitcase belonging to Mr Robert Barclay, from the lost property counter. Kennedy left Lily with his father while he went to collect the suitcase. He wondered what was in it. Not that it mattered, as he would sort it out when he felt it was the right time. All he felt now was a sense of loss. He had never talked over with his father what to do with his estate as they thought he still had more years left, but this was not to be.

When he arrived back, the doctor was examining the deceased body and it didn't take him long to diagnose the cause of death, a fatal heart attack. His father would not have known or felt anything as it happened so quick, which was a blessing. This brought a little comfort to Kennedy knowing he hadn't suffered. They waited until the hearse arrived to take his father's body away.

Lily felt she could not leave Kennedy on his own, so she went back to his home with him. She made him a coffee and they sat and chatted. He needed company as this loss had hit him really hard.

It wasn't until Lily's cell phone rang that she realised how time had flown and it was getting late. "When are you coming home, Lily? The children need to go to bed; they are grizzly," was what greeted her.

"Can't you shower them and put them to bed? It is part of your duty as their father," she told him.

Reece got a shock as he had never been spoken to like this before by Lily. "It's not my job. I earn the money, and you are their mother, Lily."

Once again, her buttons were pushed to the limit, so she answered him back, "Don't forget I work as well as care for the children. I will be there shortly," and with this she hung up on him.

Kennedy heard this conversation and was angry at the way Reece talked to Lily. "He doesn't deserve you, my darling," he said in all sincerity. Kennedy asked Lily if she would help him go through his father's belongings, when Reece had returned to Auckland.

Lily's home welcome was not as she would have wished, as the children were still up playing with their toys while Reece was on his cell phone. She bypassed him and took the twins to the bathroom for a shower and then helped them into their pyjamas, ready for bed. Once this was all done, she told them to say 'goodnight' to their father and Reece acknowledged this by a wave of his hand while he continued talking on his phone.

Leila showered herself; she was a big girl as she only had two weeks to go until she started school. When she finished, she went and gave her father a kiss while he was still consumed with his phone conversation. This showed Lily just how important the children were to him!

She put the toys away and cleaned up the dishes then went to bed. She must have dropped off to sleep before Reece came to bed as it was 7.30am when she woke. Today was Saturday so she didn't have to go to work, but she got up and dressed as Reece was still asleep. Their nanny had the weekends off, so this was family time for Lily, which she loved.

Lily had an early dinner as Reece was going to a meeting at Lincoln's pad. He still hadn't told her what it was about, so she only knew from what Kennedy had told her. Things were very cool at home and no discussions were forthcoming.

As Reece drove to Lincoln's, he had time to think about his and Lily's relationship. It was on shaky ground at the moment and he couldn't think why this had happened. Perhaps she needed to give up work and become a full-time mother. He would suggest this to her before he left for Auckland. Kennedy's vehicle was already at Lincoln's pad, so he pulled up behind it. He was keen to know what was happening on the crypto front. He realised he had not had time to offer Kennedy his condolences so he would do so before they got down to business. As he entered Lincoln's pad that old feeling of friendship flowed back through his veins, it was good to be part of the lads again, and he realised he had missed this. They sat around and talked about Kennedy's father as they had had a lot to do with him over the past few years.

Now it was down to business. Into the computer room they went all eager to see what fortunes lay ahead. They pulled their chairs up to the computer and watched in anticipation as Lincoln opened their bitcoin wallet. The news was not good, as the bitcoin had slid further down, eroding their fortunes by 20 per cent. This had happened in six weeks, such is the volatility of the crypto world. Next week it could shoot up again, but as agreed, today was D-Day.

Now it was time to cross over to see how the OpenSea platform was performing. Their NFTs auction was finished so it was time to see what the closing bid was. They had spent $1 million on the 'crypto-punk' artwork and it had fetched $2.5 million. Not a big gain, but a little was better than a loss. NFTs trading had treated them kindly as it seemed to be the investment of the moment. Kennedy pointed out he was surprised that this was the case, as the rate at which bitcoin is created, it is reduced every four years, a process called halving, so the bitcoin supply is dwindling, which should have added to its demand. Perhaps this was to happen in the future, something for him and Lincoln to look forward to.

Now it was down to the nitty-gritty, the three-way split. Their bitcoin split had been reduced from $70 million a share to $56 million by the 20 per cent decline. Now they could finalise the NFTs investment. For the investment of $6.2 million they had made $23.5 million, a profit of $17.3 million, so a three-way split netted them roughly $5.8 million each. This was the amount they first invested into cryptocurrency, so the crypto world had made them into millionaires many times over. Their goal was to become billionaires, which lasted for a short time, but here they were today very wealthy young men with a bright future ahead of them!

Reece wanted all his money out as he was on the lookout for a hotel of his own. He would stay where he was until he had the experience needed. He told the lads that he and Lily would operate the hotel together. Kennedy listened in silence, wondering if Reece had discussed this with Lily.

Lincoln's eyes went directly to Kennedy. How would he take this news now that he knew about the affair between Lily and Kennedy?

Kennedy decided to withdraw $10 million to replace the money he had given Lily for her share of the law firm. The balance he would leave in cryptocurrencies, as, like Lincoln, he enjoyed the buzz of the crypto world. Lincoln also decided to withdraw $10 million to buy himself a nice home as he had outgrown his bachelor pad. He wanted to set up a proper computer system that could be viewed from anywhere in the room, rather than them all having to squeeze around a small screen. He felt he deserved to have a splash out on his favourite pastime, being the complete computer nerd that he was. He lived for it and was always on his computer, and this suited the arrangement he had with his partner, as neither wanted to be completely committed to each other. They came and went as suited their needs.

Next was the big question! Reece asked Kennedy what he wanted from life, as he still didn't seem interested in dating. Lincoln listened with interest to his answer.

"I haven't thought much about the future, I'll just take it as it comes," he answered.

"By the way, Kennedy," said Reece, "did your father have any grandchildren? I heard the medic at the airport talking to Lily and asking her how the grandchildren would handle their grandfather's death."

Kennedy hesitated, and it was Lincoln who came to the rescue, trying to switch subjects. "Have you got a hotel in mind you are looking at?" he asked Reece.

"Yes, I have my eye on one on the outskirts of Auckland."

"Has Lily seen it?" he enquired.

"No, I will make the decision. Lily doesn't know much about the hospitality industry, so she will just have to accept the one I choose."

Kennedy had to bite his tongue, but he thought how selfish Reece had become; he didn't deserve Lily.

"Right, Kennedy, have you done your homework on New Zealand's tax reform?" asked Lincoln.

Kennedy told them that the Inland Revenue Department's view on the taxing of cryptocurrency was that there were no special rules, but that would change now that technology was rapidly evolving. The department – the IRD – is considering whether the current law taxes crypto transactions appropriately, so it is a work in progress.

There is a way of evading tax Kennedy had learnt and

that was to invest in gold, be it in coins, cast or minted bars, but it had to be at least 99.5 per cent pure gold. In most countries investing in gold is free of value-added tax, and it is not subjected to annual taxes or taxed as part of your income.

"I don't know what you want to do, Reece, when you change your cryptocurrency for money. Your share from the wallet can be directed to cash, which will then be deposited into your bank account. Also, some bitcoin ATMs let you convert bitcoin from your wallet into cash, when you scan your wallet QR code and enter the amount. If we sell through an exchange service we are interacting with a regulated business and they have to comply with anti-money laundering regulations so as to prevent criminal activities and tax evasion. Because cryptocurrency is a relatively new 'revolution' it needs to be regulated, so in time new laws will be put in place and new taxes will be introduced. The banks will make sure of this because at the moment they are the big losers."

"There is also 'Coinloan', an all-in-one crypto platform that lets you trade, lend or borrow and earn interest on various cryptocurrencies. Perhaps you could look into this if you are not going to use the money straight away. Although, once again, it can be volatile, so if you don't want any worries of the up and down fluctuations, it's best you cash it in and put it somewhere safe," advised Kennedy.

"Yes, I want it to be available, so no more crypto investments for me," he replied.

"I know bond yields are currently being outpaced by inflation so stay away from them," Kennedy advised.

Lincoln opened a bottle of champagne to celebrate the end of the threesome's crypto investments. It had been an exciting, as well as a nerve-racking, ride at times, but youth was on their side, and whatever happened, they still had earning capacity ahead of them. Lincoln and Kennedy would stay involved in the crypto world, but both wanted to invest separately to see what fortunes lay ahead. Lincoln would still have to continue with the computer work for Kennedy as he was the one handling the crypto wallet.

As the wine flowed talk turned to politics, a subject that always turned controversial. This got Kennedy heated so he expressed his views. "We vote for people to make decisions for us … that's democracy for you! I hate politics, I don't vote. I want to make my own decisions, and if I mess up then that's my fault. I don't like other people deciding what I should do and that's what governments do. That's why I like the crypto world, no regulations, no inflation, you ride the wave of success or you stumble and fall. But you can always find another wave as there are plenty of new ones out there."

"You know, Kennedy, you are a free spirit," said Reece. "No wonder you don't want commitments. Your life is all about you. Will you ever find someone who will share your dreams? If you don't, you will grow old on your own."

This led to bad thoughts floating through Kennedy's mind. He wasn't going to be the lonely one. If Reece had bought Lily the share in her law practice she so wanted, things might have been different, but who knew what lay ahead? He never wanted to fall out with Reece but one day it was going to happen.

Lincoln listened on, not wanting to side with either of his friends; the best thing to do was remain silent.

"Come around tomorrow, Reece, and tell me how you want to collect your money. Discuss it with Lily tonight," said Lincoln.

"I will decide myself. Lily doesn't have to know the exact amount we have," he retorted.

Lincoln was surprised by his remark and let it slide. They had been drinking and personal matters were delicate to handle at the best of times. Kennedy was disgusted with Reece's remark and was happy the threesome was being reduced to a twosome. Guilt was looming over him, even more so now that his and Reece's relationship was closer than what they could have imagined. "What time do you fly out on Monday?" asked Kennedy.

"On the same flight as last time, 3 o'clock," Reece replied.

"That's great, it will give you time to spend with the children; they will like that."

Reece said he had got out of the way of the children's noise as he lived in his own suite in the hotel where everything was quiet. "To be truthful I am glad to escape after a couple of days. It's good to get back to just Natalia and me." This raised eyebrows. Who was Natalia?

Today being Sunday, Kennedy felt it was time to

unpack his father's suitcase. It had been sitting in the corner of his lounge and all he could do up until now was look at it. He had just got off the phone to his sister, and they had been reminiscing on their life as youngsters. She was happy she had spent time taking her father places as it was his first holiday abroad. "You know, Kennedy, as I think about Father's health, there were several days when he was so tired, he retired to bed straight after his evening meal. Perhaps this was the build-up to his heart attack. I will have happy memories of our time together," she told him.

She went on to mention that their father had told her about their long-lost mother, and she was grateful to Kennedy for looking after her in her final weeks. A hidden truth had not been revealed, as Kennedy's sister was the result of an affair while married to his father, so this made her his half-sister.

"Yes, I'm happy I could do that for her. She was homeless and penniless, and it ripped my heart open to hear of her sad life. Even Father came to visit her. Did he tell you about my friend Reece? That was a huge shock, as he is also your half-brother, but that is not the end, because we have twins out there somewhere."

It was the mention of twins that opened the door for his sister to question him. "You are a dark horse. Father told me about your predicament. What are you going to do, Kennedy? He said you love your twins and that you are a hands-on father to them, and he was very proud of you for this."

Hearing these words filled Kennedy with pride. He

knew what he wanted to do, but when and how was the burning question. This phone conversation with his sister put him in the right frame of mind to get on and unpack the suitcase.

Tears flowed as he laid his father's clothes in piles beside his suitcase. He found little treasures his father had bought, perhaps reminders of places he had been, but now of course he didn't need them. Once all the clothes were unpacked, he found three presents with tags on: Leila, Mackenzie and Harrison. Kennedy loved that his father remembered Leila as well as his own grandchildren. He would ask Lily to bring the children around tomorrow after work as then Reece would be on his way to Auckland. They could have a takeaway tea together and he could give them their presents.

He loved family time, and he was more of a family man than Reece. It was only then he remembered Reece's words, 'It's good to get back to just Natalia and myself'. At the time, neither he nor Lincoln had queried Reece about this statement as it was so unexpected. Was it a slip of the tongue? Surely, he didn't mean to let this out? Perhaps Natalia was a pet and they were barking up the wrong tree? Would Lily know of Natalia? He would ask her.

Lily was hoping that because it was Sunday perhaps they could all go to the park as a family, as Reece would be gone tomorrow. When she mentioned this to him, he told her he had a meeting with Lincoln.

"But, Reece, we need time together as a family. You have hardly spent any time with the children."

He told her business came first as he only had today to organise his finances.

"What finances?" Lily asked.

She knew, but as yet he had not discussed it with her. It was then he told her he was taking his money out of his crypto investments. "I am looking for a nice hotel of our own, then we can all live together, and you can help me manage it," he told her.

"But I've told you, Reece, hotels are not my scene. I want to be a High Court Judge and that will be the goal of my career. I want you to pursue your dream, but I won't be part of it. Surely we can work it so that we both have the careers we want?"

This left Reece shocked, as he just presumed that she would do what he wanted. "I wanted to talk to you about that, Lily. We seem to be drifting apart lately. I want you to give up work and be a full-time mother to our children."

This was when Lily saw red. "No, Reece, I will not give up my job. I love what I do: it stimulates me, it takes my mind away from the children for a few hours each day. I think I manage okay with both positions, don't I?"

Reece looked at her. Now was the time for him to be truthful. "You are cold in bed. No longer are you giving of your love, and you just turn your back. I am putting this down to you being exhausted by night-time, so something has to go."

"Reece, I only see you for three days every six weeks, and you do nothing to help with the children to lighten my load. Your love-making tactics aren't exactly what I would call romantic. You never say anything nice to me, you don't touch or seduce me any more, so don't put all the blame on me." Lily let him know how she felt.

With these words ringing in his ears, Reece told Lily he was off to Lincoln's.

Reece and Lincoln worked out what they thought was the best way to release Reece's money. If Lincoln directed it straight from the wallet into cash on current rates, then he could put it straight into Reece's bank account. It was unknown how much tax he would have to pay, as the IRD was still working on whether the existing tax rates were sufficient to apply to cryptocurrency conversions. It was all a new revelation that was still evolving. No one had looked into the future of the crypto world. It was thought of as a passing phase that would run itself out, but that's not what happened. It bucked the trend and shot to fame with the help of celebrities in the movie and music world, along with social media. They were the ones who pumped up bitcoin and especially the NFTs, as ways of bypassing taxes and inflation, in a form of retaliation … but for how long? Now the countries that did not subject bitcoin and NFTs to taxation were changing their policies, perhaps egged on by the banks who were the big losers.

Lincoln asked Reece to let him and Kennedy know how much tax he had to pay, if any, on his cashed in cryptocurrency.

Lily had seen Reece off at the airport, but their goodbyes were bitter-sweet as they had not yet dealt satisfactorily with his wish for her to give up work. She had stood staunchly on her beliefs, so it was a parting of very few words. She would pick the children up as the nanny was due to finish for the day. Then she would drive to Kennedy's home as she had a key. It didn't matter if he wasn't home yet. The children had plenty of books and games there; he catered for all their needs.

Leila picked a book for Lily to read so they all settled beside her on the settee, and this is what greeted Kennedy when he arrived. He stood and took all this in as to him this is what family was all about. "Right children, your grandfather brought you all a present back from his holiday. There is one each," and he handed out the parcels.

"Look what Grandad brought me," shouted Leila. She held up a lunch box for her school lunches; she was starting school soon. Kennedy was thrilled that his father had remembered she was nearly five, as she was not his biological granddaughter. Mackenzie unwrapped a lovely doll and Harrison was zooming around with a tip-truck. They were all happy with their presents.

On a separate chair he had put the little souvenirs his father had brought back from Canada, so he told the children to take whatever they wanted and it wasn't long before the chair was emptied. Tears filled Kennedy's eyes as he remembered telling his father that Lily's twins were his babies. At the start he was not happy, but eventually he came round, as he noticed how his son had matured and accepted his responsibilities. He could see Lily was the love of Kennedy's life, but it all became even more complicated when they found out that he and Reece were half-brothers.

Suddenly the doorbell rang and their ordered

takeaways had arrived. They all sat around the table as a family with their separate food orders. The children loved it when they could get what they wanted. Kennedy sat opposite Lily and couldn't help brushing his leg against hers, as just to touch her sent tingles through his body. She responded by running her foot up his leg, thus the beginning of a secret liaison beneath the table. They could not show their affection in the open in front of the children, so this was a substitute. Kennedy wished they could be together like this forever, and perhaps that day wasn't too far off.

On Monday morning, Kennedy received a phone call from his father's lawyer asking him to come to his office to discuss his father's will. Kennedy had no idea of his father's personal wealth. All he had done was make sure his father didn't want for anything. He knew he owned his own home. Kennedy had left the funeral arrangements as he had no idea what his father wanted, but it was all there in the will. He wanted to be cremated and his ashes to be put in his wife's burial plot. This was a total shock to Kennedy, as he knew his mother had deeply hurt his father when she walked out on the family. Written down was the reason for his wish: she had had a sad life and he didn't want her to be alone any more, so now she would have someone with her.

Kennedy had to fight to hold back his tears. All those years his father suffered and held on to his bitterness, but now he wanted to be with her again. Perhaps his bitterness was really love and he had misread his own feelings. Kennedy was totally perplexed, but a ray of happiness shone down on him: they were reunited as a family in death.

The home was to be sold and the beneficiaries of his will were Mackenzie and Harrison, his grandchildren. This came as another surprise, but then, who else needed the money? he certainly didn't and neither did his sister, so this left the grandchildren next in line. How was this going to be administered? It would have to be kept from Reece. He would have to talk this over with Lily.

Now that he knew his father's last wishes he could go ahead and make arrangements for his funeral. They would just have a private service with invited guests only. His sister had said she wouldn't come over because of the long distance and she had spent the last three months with him, so those lovely memories would remain with her.

Several days had passed when Lily was asked to come to Kennedy's home as he wanted to talk with her. He opened a bottle of wine as he felt this was a time to celebrate. He had to tell Lily about his father leaving his estate to their children. How were they going to work around this? He waited until she had emptied her glass, then he refilled it. Now he felt the time was right. "Lily, father's lawyer rang me about his will. He has left his entire estate to Mackenzie and Harrison. They will get the money from the sale of his home and any money he had in his bank. As yet that amount hasn't been decided. This was his wish."

Lily was shocked. This was a situation she had never thought about. What would Reece say? No, Reece must never know, as this would reveal the truth. "Oh my God, how do we handle this, Kennedy?" she asked.

He had given it some thought, "Perhaps their bank accounts could be held at the lawyer's office, and therefore no statements would be issued. The bank accounts would be in their names but under the lawyer's umbrella. What do you think about that?"

Lily thought for a moment. "I would rather it be under your supervision, Kennedy. He was your father, so you can receive the statements and keep them secret. I would be happier with that," she told him.

Just as Lily was about to leave, Kennedy asked her if Reece had a pet.

"No, I don't think so. He is not a pet person, besides I don't think he would be able to have a pet at the hotel. Why do you ask?"

"He just happened to mention the name 'Natalia' to Lincoln and me."

"What did he say?"

Kennedy felt uneasy, as he didn't want to be caught up in something he may later regret. "Oh, it was mentioned in passing, probably doesn't mean anything."

It was then Lily realised that perhaps her suspicions about Reece and Natalia were true, as he spent most of his time on his cellphone to her. Would she say anything to Kennedy? No, she would keep it to herself in the meantime. Then she started to put things together. Was that why he wasn't interested in her any more?

The more Lily dwelled on this the sadder she felt. She

needed to be loved, so pleaded with Kennedy to come around to her home after she had put the children to bed.

But out of the little respect that he had left for Reece, Kennedy declined. He would not make love in Reece's home. Bad memories haunted him of what he did to Lily nearly six years ago at Reece's pad. He loved her completely, but this was a definite no-no! "Finish work early tomorrow and come around and warm my bed for me," he told her.

Moving up the ladder at work

L ily had become very popular at her work, as more than enough clients had been put her way. She found she was having to bring work home to keep up with what was expected of her, but this was not a worry as she loved the work, and it was a step closer to her goal. If Reece had been living at home, he would not have allowed this to happen, so she was happy he worked away.

Now Lily was handling a civil case against a high-profile politician where his reputation was in jeopardy. He had been falsely accused of misappropriate behaviour, that of touching a female employee. After hearing his side of the story, and having an insight into the case, she learned the accuser had been stalking the politician for six months, hoping to snare him into a relationship. He tried to make her work position untenable, hoping she would bow out gracefully, but no, she was there for the kill.

Lily spoke to the people surrounding the accuser at work and it was general knowledge that she was out to have a fling with him. She had told several of them that she wanted to have an affair. After much deliberation she was deemed an unreliable witness, so it all ended in tears. She lost her job and any chance of an affair with the politician. This was the best-case scenario for Lily, as the politician was most grateful and said if he could help her with anything in the future, he would be happy to do so. This she would keep up her sleeve, and if she needed a person of high integrity then this was her man!

It wasn't long until Lily was asked to handle a huge libel case, which would enable her to appear in the High Court, where cases involving amounts over $350 as well as criminal cases were heard. This would allow her to move up in the system, so although she was nervous, she had to take the opportunity when it arose.

Leila was a big girl now as she was off to school with her new lunch box which her grandad had brought back from Canada and a school bag, which her father had bought her. He couldn't come to her party, but Uncle Kennedy was there! Lily took the day off work and drove her to school, to be there for her in case any problems arose, but this was unfounded, as she found friends as soon as she entered the school grounds.

She decided to call Reece and tell him how it all went. She rang his private number and the phone was answered by a woman. "Hello, Natalia speaking. Can I help you?" this was the cue for her to hang up. Now her suspicions were telling her that Natalia was definitely Reece's lover. Not that the thought of him having a lover upset her, as it was really a reprieve, but why didn't he make his daughter's birthday; this was his family responsibility. Lily was dreading his next visit, although he hadn't mentioned about them shifting up to Auckland as yet. Now that Leila was enrolled at school they would not be going anywhere. This was the lever she needed.

One month had passed and Leila was loving school. The twins were attending play-group in the mornings so everyone seemed happy. Lily's libel case was coming to an end. She did well for her client who won his claim against a former company who were in the breach for unsafe work practices. She left the High Court and returned to her law office, only to find Reece sitting there waiting for her. This was a shock as he had not told her he was coming home. She greeted him, "Hi, Reece, this is a surprise. What are you doing back here?"

Reece stared at her before asking, "What is your name doing on that plaque as a partner in the firm?"

Lily had completely forgot about the plaque and she just didn't notice it any more, as she knew in her own mind that she was a partner in the company. What could she say?

Lily never expected Reece to visit her at her workplace. This was a first, so she was caught unprepared. "I bought the share on offer. You wouldn't buy it, so I arranged my own finance. I begged you to think about it, but you made it known you weren't interested, so here I am!"

Reece was furious that Lily had gone behind his back, but he realised this was not the place to make a scene. "I'll see you at home," were his passing words.

Lily sat down at her desk and took a deep breath and closed her eyes. This was not a good start to Reece's visit. Would she tell him that Kennedy had lent her the money? No, it really wasn't any of his business. It had happened, and that was the end of it. She wondered what reception she would arrive home to.

As Lily walked in after work, the nanny was ready to leave. She had the evening meal prepared, and now it was her time with the children. "Have you seen Reece?" she asked.

"No, is he home?"

He obviously hadn't arrived yet. Lily talked to Leila about her day at school, then asked Mackenzie and Harrison how their day went. She always found time each day when she arrived home to talk to the children, as she felt this was important. If there were any problems then they could be talked about. Now it was time to serve their dinner as they were hungry little critters! She would put Reece's dinner aside and reheat it when he arrived. It wasn't until the children were in bed that Lily heard a car pull into the driveway. She was fully expecting Reece to be angry, and he did not disappoint.

"You knew, Lily, how I felt about you owning a share in your law firm, then to find your name on that plaque... What the hell are you trying to prove?"

Lily stood defiant. "It was my doing, Reece. I had the chance to buy so I took it! Nothing you say is going to change anything, so just accept it."

He was furious with Lily's reply, but he knew it was pointless to argue further.

"Your dinner is in the oven," she told him as she made her way to the bedroom. She had a shower and climbed into bed as she was tired and angry. When she woke, she was in the bed on her own. It wasn't until she dressed and walked out to the lounge that she found Reece asleep on the settee. She woke him and told him to go to their bed before the children woke up. She hadn't told them he was back, as they would get excited only to be let down by him. She would get them organised before the nanny arrived and they could see him tonight.

Reece had a meeting with Lincoln and Kennedy to tell them how he got on with the IRD while cashing in on his crypto investment. Natalia was looking after the hotel for the night so he had caught a flight down to meet up with the lads. They met at Lincoln's new home in his newly set-up high-tech computer room, which housed the most up-to-date computer and all its components. He had certainly not spared any costs as this was going to be his workplace due to the spread of the Covid virus. He hadn't had it as yet and was going to keep away from it, by working from home. Most of his work colleagues had gone down with it, so this frightened him. It was a new era and many companies were applying the same rules, to keep their workforce working from home, as then productivity continued. The next revolution in technology had arrived.

The adaptability of humans has come to the fore, as the pandemic certainly forced a shift for people to work from home, and it was becoming an integral part of the everyday workforce.

"My God, Lincoln, you certainly have a fabulous setup. You always talked about a new computer room, and you've done yourself proud," Reece praised him. Now there was no huddling in front of a small screen. The new computer data was fed into a large screen that almost commandeered the whole of the back wall. As Lincoln lay back in his lazy-boy chair, he signalled to the lads to sit in their special chairs. This was certainly luxury, and the lads were soaking up their crypto wealth.

"How are the family?" asked Lincoln. Reece elected to tell him that he had spent the night on the settee as he and Lily had argued. "I went around to Lily's office yesterday and was angry to see her name on the plaque outside the office, as a partner in the law firm."

"Why would you be angry, Reece? I would be so proud if it was my wife's name on the plaque," said Kennedy.

Reece then proceeded to tell them she had asked for the money to buy the share, but he refused, as he wanted her to be a full-time mother to his children.

"Lily is a very intelligent lady, and one day she will achieve her dream to become a High Court Judge. From our quiz days, she talked of working her way up the court ladder right to the top. Remember her dream, Reece?" Kennedy reminded him. He had never forgotten.

Lincoln listened as Reece and Kennedy went head to head. "But she has our three children to care for, that's where her priority should be," argued Reece. Kennedy went on to tell him that she was a caring mother, and he should respect that. Now it was time for Lincoln to intervene, as this was starting to get serious, and he was afraid secrets would be let out if they continued. A change of subject was needed. "Right, Reece, how did you go with the IRD? How much did they sting you?" he asked.

Reece explained they were still working on what tax to implement, as no guidelines had been set for the crypto conversions, so it was still in limbo. So, the lads were no further ahead!

Reece had booked his return flight for 6.30pm so he would go home and see his children for a few hours, then drive to the airport in the rental car. He wasn't sure if Lily would be home before he left, but he wasn't worried after what had happened last night. As he pulled up his driveway, he saw the nanny with Leila and the twins as she had picked her up from school. The children ran to their father hoping to be picked up and hugged, but this did not happen. He asked them how their day went and took their outstretched hands and walked inside with them. He then asked the nanny to make him a cup of coffee. The chatter was full on, which Reece wasn't used to, and it was too much.

"I just have to go outside and make a phone-call," he told them. He took his coffee with him and went out on to the patio and made his call. "Hi Natalia…" One hour later he returned just in time to say his goodbyes as he had to drive to the airport.

"Don't go, Daddy," pleaded Leila. Then the tears started.

"I'll be back in six weeks to see you again," he told them.

The nanny was perplexed: why did he not stay to see Lily?

"Bye children," he called as he got into the car. It was only ten minutes later that Lily arrived home.

"Mummy, Daddy has gone away again," cried an upset Leila.

Lily wondered where he had gone, and it wasn't until the nanny told what had happened that she fully understood the situation. This left her furious!

Kennedy had stayed on at Lincoln's, the two of them browsing the net to see if any new get-rich-quick schemes were out there. Lincoln was very interested in the new 'Metaverse' talk, so he explained it to Kennedy. It was not yet implemented, but it wasn't far off. The goal of the metaverse and why it is being created is to bring about the next evolution of social connection where users can interact, engage and socialise with one another in a 3D space. Because of the new work culture, office meetings were being replaced with Zoom meetings. With metaverse you put on a VR headset or AR glasses and you will be transported to a virtual office, all without leaving the comfort of your own home. It brings the internet to life; you can go inside instead of looking at a screen.

The mere mention of it not yet being available made Kennedy sit up and take note. It all sounded so futuristic, but then so did the crypto platform until he became involved. He knew the whiz kids of today were right into what the future could hold, as they wanted challenges and excitement. The old world that belonged to their parents had had its day, that era had passed, and now there was a new horizon awaiting! Was this the new money spinner?

To Kennedy, this possibility smelt of money! Lincoln had been invited into an exciting niche called the 'GameFi' gaming guild, which allowed him to join talented players in the 'play-to-earn' realm. They used the highest-quality NFTs to improve their game performance and were able to generate additional income. His knowledge as a computer programmer earned him this invitation, and because he was experienced in NFTs this was a bonus. Now he was entering into the next-generation social network and internet platform.

Lincoln wanted Kennedy to come along for the ride as he knew he was an entrepreneur and well respected in the financial sector. Two brains working together, each with knowledge in different but connected fields, was surely a winning team. Kennedy could see the potential, as gaming among the young would become more engaging and immersive, just what they were looking for. Lincoln realised that the metaverse could be a shared interaction environment, where both physical and digital worlds collide.

Lincoln and Kennedy were still dabbling in cryptocurrency and NFTs, so they were surprised to see in the news there had been a recent explosion in the blockchain ecosystem. The biggest boost was when the co-owner of the largest social networking website changed the company's name to 'Meta', thus reaching the mainstream public's awareness. It had become the latest buzz word to catch the tech industry's imagination.

"It's not easy for ordinary people who are not computer savvy to enter into the digital world of NFTs. It needs to be made useful to the everyman, rather than just to the technologically savvy, the computer corporates and the ultra-rich," announced Kennedy. "It is not an equal playing field at the moment. Currently absent are fractional ownerships and user-friendly minting, storage and purchasing capabilities," he continued. Lincoln agreed, but was now the time to develop a more user-friendly platform for the public to participate? Was this the cue they needed?

Lincoln could understand why Reece found all this hard to digest, thus making him feel uncomfortable and out of sorts, especially with the NFTs. That he had decided to cash in his cryptocurrency made Lincoln happy, as if not for his family's inheritance, they would not have made it onto the millionaire bracket. Reece now had his money, so he could start looking to buy his own hotel. Lincoln was perplexed as to why Reece had not bought the share in the law firm that Lily so wanted, as it wasn't as if the finance was a problem.

He had noticed a change in Reece since he was appointed as hotel manager of the Auckland property, and this saddened him a little. They were good friends regardless of their level of intelligence, but this was always a big thing with Reece. And when he found out his true background, he tried even harder to prove his ability. He could see why Lily had turned to Kennedy, as he was a generous-hearted soul who loved the children and would do anything for them. Not that he was always this person. When he told Lincoln he had bedded Lily against her will and that he was remorseful for his self-indulgence, this was the turning point in his life. He had forgiven Kennedy, as he was fond of him, and they were of equal intelligence and had a deep yearning to succeed in life.

Their meeting was interrupted by a phone call; it was Lily on the other end. She seemed upset and asked Kennedy to please come to her home as she needed him. Lincoln overheard this conversation and told Kennedy to go to her.

When Kennedy arrived, Lily was in tears. She was deeply hurt that Reece hadn't told her he was there for just one night, and now he was gone! The nanny had told her he hadn't spent much time with the children, that he was on the phone for an hour.

"You know when you asked about the name 'Natalia', twice I have called Reece on his private number and she has answered his phone. I think they must be sleeping together, not that it worries me, but I would like to know, and if so, I can make some decisions on my own life. We had an argument about my name being on the plaque outside the law office," Lily sobbed. "I would have hoped he would be proud of me, but instead I don't think he liked it."

Kennedy took her in his arms and held her close to him. "If you were my wife, I would be so proud of you, Lily. We all knew from that first meeting at the quiz night what your intentions were for your future, and Reece should have respected that, as you are a very intelligent lady. It was my biggest regret that I was so self-centred and didn't realise that you were the very one I was looking for, but Reece beat me. Perhaps this is the time to find the truth as to who Natalia is. Would you fly to Auckland unannounced and surprise Reece?" he asked.

Lily said she couldn't leave the children; it was then Kennedy suggested that he and the nanny would look after them.

The surprise visit

Lily had arrived in Auckland and was in a taxi on her way to the inner-city hotel. She felt a little apprehensive about her visit, but the hurt was still there in her heart. She had reserved a room for the night under an assumed name, hoping Reece didn't see her while she was booking in. The taxi pulled up at the entrance and she alighted, all the time looking to see that Reece was nowhere to be seen. She walked up to reception and gave her name and filled out the paperwork, then was given a room key. A bellboy took her suitcase to her room and opened the door and put her case on the suitcase rack. She asked him if the manager lived on the premises.

"Yes, his suite is on the ground floor off the hallway behind the office."

Lily thanked him and he wished her a happy stay, then left. Lily unpacked and had a shower as she had time to fill in. It was 6pm. She could not be seen in the dining area so came prepared with her homemade sandwiches. Now that she knew where Reece's suite was, she would wait until the office closed then pay him a visit. She studied the compendium and found the office hours: the hotel operated from 6.30am till 10pm.

She called Kennedy to see that the children were okay and they talked for thirty minutes. He told her the nanny had showered them before he arrived and she had prepared their dinner, so he fed them, then read them their goodnight stories.

"That's what I love about you, Kennedy. Nothing is a worry; you just get on with the job. I know you love Leila and the twins, and they love you in return. It is sad that Reece has lost interest in them. I think since he arrived in Auckland he has got used to the peace and quiet. I wonder what I will find later," she said.

Kennedy told her he loved her, no matter the outcome, and that he would be there for her. "Thank you, my love, I will see you tomorrow. Love you," she replied.

It was just past 10.30 when Lily made her way to the office and followed the hallway until she saw the sign on the door, 'Manager's Suite'. She knocked and waited. The door opened and there stood a young lady in her pyjamas. She looked at Lily. "Who are you?" she asked.

"Is Reece here? I need to speak to him," said Lily.

"He has just gone to do a final lock-up. I'll tell him you called. What is your name?" she asked.

Lily asked if she could come in as she would wait for him. The young lady invited Lily in, thinking something was wrong. "Are you staying in the hotel?" she asked. It was then the door opened and in walked Reece.

"Lily, what are you doing here?" he asked in horror.

"Who is this young lady?" Lily asked.

Reece was caught out and he felt embarrassed.

"You don't need to explain. I know she is Natalia. When I have called you, she has answered your private phone. I just came to see what I had suspected, and now I know. I will fly home tomorrow. Goodbye, Reece."

With this Lily opened the door and left. Reece was still in shock and by the time realisation hit, he ran to the door, but Lily had gone. Of course, he couldn't make contact with her as she was staying under an assumed name, not that he knew this. He went straight to the office and looked through the guest register, but Lily's name was nowhere to be found.

The next morning as Lily came down to the reception to pay, there was Reece waiting for her. He told the receptionist that he would fix up this guest's accommodation bill. Lily thanked him and walked to the door.

"Lily, please listen to me, I'm sorry. You should have told me you were coming," he told her.

"Then you would have got rid of her for the night and I would know no different. I have heard you on the phone to her when you have come home, Reece. I'm not silly; I knew you had someone else. I just wish you had told me. I need time to think about us, now that I know the truth. We can discuss this next time you come home."

It was then Reece knew it was all over. He hadn't

wanted Lily to find out this way, but he couldn't bring himself to tell her he had fallen in love with someone else. Natalia and Reece had declared their love for each other and were looking at a hotel to purchase that they could operate together. They both shared the same love for the hospitality industry, whereas Lily didn't.

He realised he would have to fly home before his six-week stint and sort things out with Lily as she would be heartbroken. She wasn't the girl he fell in love with, and once the children came along things were different. He thought being a father would be fun, but being an only child, he was not used to the constant chatter – it was something he hadn't experienced. He loved the children, but he still needed time away. He missed Leila most as she told him she missed him, but the twins were younger and less interested. It wasn't until he moved to Auckland that he realised how much he needed his privacy and his own space.

Natalia didn't want children of her own so she and Reece would share custody of his children with Lily. He did wonder how Kennedy and Lincoln would accept this, as Lily had been part of their lives for over eight years, since the quiz days.

Reece had let Lily know he was arriving this afternoon and would pick up a rental car at the airport to save her driving out, as she would have to take time off work. The nanny would be looking after the children until Lily came home. He decided his first call would be to Lincoln's home. He knew Lily would have told the lads about their situation and he wondered how it would affect their friendship. Not that he was really worried as he had made it to the top of his profession so now considered himself equal to them.

In Lincoln and Kennedy's minds, it didn't matter that he wasn't as intelligent as them; it was all in his head. They never forgot he was the one that shared his inheritance, so to them he was every bit an equal partner.

Reece knocked on Lincoln's door and waited for him to answer. When he opened the door, he welcomed Reece with their usual high-five. They talked about Lincoln's new technology set-up and how he preferred working from home, away from all the viruses that were floating in the air. He even did his food shopping online like many other people.

Lincoln explained to Reece that he had been listening to a podcast and a bank's chief economist said the pandemic had condensed the shift online, which was expected to take up to a decade, into little more than one year, and he expected this would lead to an online shopping explosion! This was how quick the world was adjusting to the new high-tech world. The positives were convenience, time saving, and comparing competitors' prices all from the comfort of the home.

But this came with a warning, as with positives come negatives – people becoming sedentary, lazy and withdrawing from interacting with others. Lincoln thought in fact it could be the beginning of a metaverse evolution in social connection, like the internet but more immersive.

Reece found this all a little above him, but it did sound exciting. There was no mention of his and Lily's problem. Lincoln did not want to become involved as he knew more than Reece, especially about the affair.

Lily told the children their father was coming home tonight and as always Leila was excited, wanting to know if he was going to stay forever. She showered them before dinner to allow Reece to spend quality time with them. They waited, but hungry little tummies won out, so Lily decided to serve up their meal. It was then they heard a car pull up into the driveway and minutes later Reece appeared at the door. They ran to him expecting to be picked up, but this did not happen. It was not Kennedy; this was their father.

Reece spoke to them and ruffled their hair as he passed and greeted Lily. The atmosphere was a little strained as their last meeting had not been very amicable. "Dinner is ready. Let's all sit down and eat as a family," said Lily. Mackenzie and Harrison were sitting next to each other, and Leila sat by her father. Then the chatter started, the twins started poking each other, causing an argument, Leila was full on capturing her father's attention, silence had vanished and chaos reigned. This was the norm for Lily but for Reece it was too much. "Can we have a little silence while we eat?" he asked. This brought a response from Leila: "But, Daddy, we always talk at the table, don't we, Mummy?"

"Your father is not used to noise so please do as he asks," replied Lily.

After they finished eating Leila asked her father to read them a story, which he did without protesting.

Once Lily and Reece had the lounge to themselves it was time for them to talk. Reece started. "I'm sorry that you found out about Natalia the way you did, as it must have been a shock for you. I don't know what has happened to us. Perhaps if you had come to Auckland with me at the beginning, we may still have been together. It wasn't until I had my own suite that I realised how much I missed living without the constant noise of the children. I love them, Lily, and I am really disappointed in myself. Where do we go from here?"

Lily thought for a moment. "First, we have to start with the home. The children have to have somewhere to live."

Reece said he would sign the house over to her and put $1 million in her bank account. She didn't know how much he had cashed his cryptocurrency for, as he had never talked about it with her, but she knew it would have been a good sum of money. She would wait and ask Kennedy, as he would know. She was pleased that he had bought her the share in the law firm as she was receiving a dividend as well as her wage. Reece had never asked her about her work, so he had no idea what she was earning.

"I've talked to Natalia about the children. She doesn't want any of her own, so she is happy to share custody with me of our children. We will draw up an agreement and I will work out when it suits us to have them. I'm sorry it has come to this, Lily, as I thought we were going to be forever soulmates, but we shared some good times so let us not forget them. I'm sure Lincoln and Kennedy will look after you," he said. "How are we going to tell the children? Perhaps I will leave it up to you."

Lily had sat and listened to what he had to say and now it was all left for her, once again. She was disappointed in Reece as a father as he didn't have much input into their lives. Because of this, Lily felt when the time came for her to tell Reece about the twins belonging to Kennedy it was not going to be as heart-breaking as she thought. But when was that time? Here the conversation came to an end, so Lily said goodnight to Reece and went to bed. He curled up on the settee, as this was his bed for the night, although he had hoped Lily would let him sleep in their bed for the last time, but, no, the invitation was not forthcoming!

Today Reece was going to take the children to McDonald's for lunch then to the playground, to give Lily a break, as he was flying back to Auckland in the morning. This was a good escape for Lily as it was Saturday and Kennedy would be home, so she would drive around and offer to warm his bed. It had been over a week since their last rendezvous and she was missing him, and she longed for him to make love to her. Just to hear his passionate talk as he made love was the best feeling ever. It made her feel as if she was the only woman alive! Sometimes she would think back to the first time he bedded her, which had been against her will, but even then he was gentle and declared his love for her between his apologies of self-indulgence. Had that been the real beginning of her feelings for Kennedy?

When Reece left with the children, Lily changed her clothes and put makeup on, then drove around to Kennedy's home. He was cleaning his car when she arrived, but that could wait, as now he had another appointment to keep. They rushed inside straight to the bedroom where they shed their clothes and jumped in under the duvet. Both sets of hands roamed under the bedclothes, touching places of interest until it all became too much. The sweettalk had worked its magic, and Lily begged to be taken. She needed to have him right now, at this very moment! She was not disappointed; never had she been loved so completely.

Later, as they lay there, Lily asked him how much money Reece would have collected when he cashed in his cryptocurrency. "We all got an even share of over $60 million. Did he not tell you?" he asked.

Lily told him that Reece was signing the home over to her and he would put $1 million in her bank account.

"That is so unfair, Lily. I would give you every penny I owned. What did you say?"

"I just listened as I didn't know how much he had. He is drawing up a custody roster for joint parenting of the children."

"This is where I am putting my foot down, Lily. I don't want someone I don't know looking after the twins. You are their mother and a loving one at that. What do we know about this Natalia?" he asked.

Suddenly she realised the dilemma that was now

facing her. Kennedy being the twins' father had a right to have his say on their wellbeing. She could see the time was nearing when the truth would have to be revealed.

Lily told Kennedy she would help him finish cleaning his car as payment for two blissful hours in his bed. As they were hosing it down Reece arrived with the children. This was a surprise, but then he hadn't seen Kennedy this visit.

"What are you doing here?" he asked Lily.

She explained she had to give Kennedy a message so ended up helping him clean his car.

"Hi kids," called Kennedy. This was the signal to run to him and he would lift them all up together. He pretended to be the strongman in the circus. They loved him, as he was so interactive with them.

This went right over Reece's head. Kennedy was then roped into a game of tag, until Lily offered to take the children home in her car so Reece and Kennedy could have time to themselves. They grizzled as they wanted to stay, but Lily's loud tone told them otherwise.

Now it was time for the lads to catch up on what was happening in their lives. Reece started the conversation by telling Kennedy about his future aspirations. "I'm looking at a newly constructed hotel on the outskirts of Auckland. We are in negations with the developers and we should know within the fortnight if it is ours. It will not be available for four months, so in the meantime I will gain more experience. Natalia and I are really excited about our new adventure together."

Kennedy couldn't help himself. "What happened between you and Lily?"

Reece told him it didn't work out as Lily had changed; she had put her career before the children.

Kennedy immediately went on the defensive: "But, Reece, you always knew what Lily's aspirations were. To say she put her career first is simply not true. Her children have always come first. I'm disappointed to hear you say otherwise."

"There hasn't been much affection between us for a while. Perhaps if she had come up to Auckland with me at the start, we may have been able to rekindle our relationship, but now it is too late, as I have met Natalia. Lily was never interested in the hospitality industry, whereas Natalia loves it," responded Reece.

Kennedy asked how Reece thought the children would feel about what was going to happen. Reece told him that he and Natalia were drawing up a custody agreement which he hoped Lily would sign.

"But they have never met her. Does Lily know anything about her background? You just can't take them away to a new environment and a new stepmother," he argued.

Reece started to get a little agitated with Kennedy, as this was none of his business. "Don't worry about our situation. Lily and I will sort it out," Reece told him.

Kennedy was angry with Reece. Was it time for the truth to come out in the open? He couldn't let it finish here. "I will worry and have my say, as Mackenzie and

Harrison are my children, and I will not agree to them staying with someone I don't know."

This statement hit Reece like a lightning bolt. "What do you mean, they are your children?"

"Lily and I had an affair and a DNA test put me as their father, but Leila is your daughter," Kennedy told him.

"You are my half-brother so this cannot be true," yelled Reece.

"This happened long before we found out about our mother. I'm sorry, Reece, but I have loved Lily right from our quiz nights. That's why I stopped dating. I couldn't satisfy anyone else, as my heart belonged to Lily."

He did not expect what came next. Reece lashed out at him and punched him in the stomach, knocking him to the ground. "You two-faced bastard," he screamed as he tried to attack him for a second time.

Kennedy jumped up and grabbed Reece's arms and twisted them behind his back. "Let us act like grown men. I know this has come as a shock to you and I'm sad you had to hear it from me, but you had to know the truth. It was when you ran Lily down about not putting her children first that I saw red. I love her, I always have and always will, but as long as you were together as husband and wife, I suffered in silence for all those years, watching you father my children. Now the truth has been revealed, you know why I am at liberty to have my say who the twins live with."

By now Reece had had time to digest what he had been confronted with, but the anger was still raw. He could not believe that Lily had let him down and for four years kept this to herself. Then he started, "I will go for full custody of Leila. Lily will not get her," he roared.

"Don't take this out on Lily, Reece. Hate me as much as you like but don't make her suffer. You can't take Leila away from her, it would break her heart. Besides the twins would miss her; they are a family."

"She has broken my heart with lies, and she will pay," retaliated Reece.

"But just a moment," said Kennedy. "What did Lily find when she came to visit you. You were having an affair behind her back. Go away and think about things before you make any stupid decisions, as it is innocent lives here, we are playing with."

As soon as Reece left, Kennedy rang Lily to warn her what had transpired between him and Reece, and that he would probably come home in a foul mood. "I'm sorry, Lily, but he was making plans for the children to stay with him and Natalia. It was too much, so the truth came out. He was so angry, I told him it was my fault and not to take it out on you. If you need me just call and I'll be there straight away. Take care, my darling!"

Now that Lily knew what to expect it gave her time to think things over, as he would arrive home shortly. But this did not happen! Instead, Reece went to Lincoln's place to tell him about Kennedy and Lily as he needed to get it out of his system. Lincoln was sympathetic as he listened to Reece's story and he did not let on he knew of the affair. He let him pour it all out.

"He is my half-brother; how could he do that to his own family member?" Reece raved on.

"But it happened before your family connection was known. We have been friends for a long time. I know it shouldn't have happened, but now you have met someone else, so make a new life for yourself and Natalia. Of course, you have a right to be angry but get over it, and don't cause a situation that one day you might regret. Sleep on it, Reece," said Lincoln.

With this, Reece burst into tears.

Lily heard the car pull into the driveway; she was nervous as she didn't know how Reece would react. As he came through the door, he roared at Lily to sit down. "What have you been up to behind my back? Tell me the truth. Who is the twins' father. I need to know."

Lily replied, "They are Kennedy's children, but Leila is your daughter. I'm sorry you had to find out from Kennedy and not from me."

Reece looked at her with hatred in his eyes. "You betrayed me, Lily, and for that I will fight for sole custody of Leila. I will take her from you and Kennedy."

"You never told me how much you sold your cryptocurrency for, then you had the audacity to put $1 million in my bank account for the care of the children. My feelings for you have dwindled. You have changed, Reece, and I don't like what I see. Kennedy was kind and caring to me and the children, he was more a hands-on person than you ever were towards them. I will not let you take Leila from me; you are entitled to have shared custody of her, but you will never get sole custody. Let us act like adults over this. You have moved on to a new partner and together you are starting a new venture, so please don't let us fall out over this. I'm sure we can come to an amicable agreement," pleaded Lily.

Reece carried on ranting and raving. "Fancy you liking Kennedy. I remember you saying he was an arrogant prick."

Lily reminded him that statement was made way back in their quiz days. "Do you know who paid for my share in the law office? Kennedy bought it for me in my name. If you had told me you sold your cryptocurrency for over $60 million, I would have expected you to buy me the share, but instead you kept that from me. Why, Reece? I was hurt that I had to learn from someone else the extent of our finances. Think about that, Reece," Lily told him.

Once the facts came out in the open Reece couldn't handle them. He turned his back and walked away. He needed time to think. First, he had to take in the fact that the twins were not his, then Lily's affair with his own flesh and blood. He felt destroyed. His own infidelity was forgotten, and all he could think of was Lily's betrayal. He was angry. Where did this leave him? He felt it was all Lily's fault, not recognising some of the blame lay with him.

The next morning Lily was up early attending the children as she didn't know what Reece's reaction would be towards Mackenzie and Harrison. Leila was not a worry as she and her father had a special bond. She wondered if he had thought about his part in all this, as he had the whole night to process what had been put in front of him. He had slept on the settee which was now unoccupied, and she could hear him on his cell phone as he was obviously out on the patio.

Lily got the children their breakfast amid the idle chatter which was common at the meal table. This was their catch-up time. "Where is Daddy?" asked Leila.

Lily told her he was talking on his cell phone, so she left the table to go and find him. They both came back together. "Mummy, make Daddy his toast," was her request, which she attended to. When her eyes met with his there was nothing there; it was like looking at a blank canvas, and their marriage was over!

Reece told the children he was leaving later in the day to return to Auckland.

"But Daddy, we don't want you to go. When will you be coming back to live with us?" sobbed Leila.

"Your mother will talk to you about that after I have gone," was his answer.

Now it was up to Lily to break the news to the children, so once again he had dodged his parental responsibilities, but this would be the last time, she told herself.

Lily was happy when Reece said his goodbyes as he had refused to discuss anything further on their broken relationship. He said it would be settled by a letter from his solicitor. She felt bitter that he wouldn't talk things over before he left, but that was his way of handling things.

She needed time to think. This was certainly a different Reece to the one she met all those years ago. She tried to think back to when the telltale signs started.

Things changed once he had met his birth mother and learned that his father was just a salesperson behind the counter in a department store. He still wanted to believe his foster parents were his family, but then again, his intelligence didn't match theirs. Where did this leave him? Was it the self-pity he had carried around most of his life, always wishing he was as intelligent as his two friends? This seemed to play on his mind, making him want to prove that he was better than what people thought, but this was only in his own mind. His friends and Lily accepted him for what he was, the guy Lily fell in love with.

It was Sunday, so Lily had the children to look after. She asked herself when the right time was to tell them. Not today, as she had to think how to break the news without the blame being put on either parent. She knew Leila would be the most affected by it, as she had a close relationship with her father. Kennedy would become the crutch the children would hold on to, as they loved him because he spent time with them most days. In fact, Lily knew they would miss him more than Reece, if he was the one leaving them.

She played with them until dinner was ready, then they sat down at the table. "When is Daddy coming back?" asked Leila. Was this the opening Lily needed? Perhaps she could try and explain as best she could.

"Daddy is buying a new hotel in Auckland so he won't be coming home very often as he will be very busy. But you will be able to go and stay with him, Leila. Would you like that?"

"But I want the twins to come with me."

Lily explained that the twins were too young, and perhaps when they were older they could go, knowing deep down this would never happen, as Kennedy had taken a stance on it.

"Oh well, we still have Uncle Kennedy to play with," Leila said.

There the conversation ended, and life continued as if nothing was going to change. Lily sighed with relief; she was expecting a barrage of questions which didn't eventuate. After the children were settled for the night, she called Kennedy on his home phone but there was no reply so she tried his cell phone. "Hi, Kennedy, can you come around tonight?"

"I'm sorry, babe, I'm around at Lincoln's, and we are tied up on his computer. Will tomorrow be okay?"

Lily felt a little sad, but she said she would see him then.

It was time for the lads to check their wallet then find out what was happening on the metaverse scene. When Lincoln updated his computer equipment, he bought new mining software. Mining is essentially 24/7 computer accounting called 'verifying' transactions. It is the workhorse known to generate substantial heat that can cook the hardware, so he used a fan to blow cool air around. Lincoln made sure that nothing could go wrong with his sophisticated equipment as he had spent a lot of money on having the most up-to-date computer components. If they were going to dabble in new experiences in the digital world, then they were ready.

Their wallet was holding out nicely, and things seemed to have stabilised in the cryptocurrency and the bitcoin was holding its own.

Now on to the metaverse! What had Lincoln found out about this new phenomenon? Kennedy was excited, as it was hot talk in financial circles and the computer-savvy kids of today were looking ahead to what could be, to an exciting world that was way beyond the ordinary one they were living in at this moment. Metaverse was definitely the next generation social network like the internet but more immersive, which brought a glimpse into what the future held.

The virtual world had arrived, as the younger generation were computer literate, they were extending the boundaries, they were becoming the leaders in technology. It would be a case of trial and error as was the case with bitcoin and NFTs, but they were making steady progress. There was still scepticism out there, but change was in the air! Middle-aged and older citizens didn't adapt to change easily, but the world was changing, having been brought about by the unwanted and unexpected pandemic.

Was this the first of more to follow?

The lads realised that being in the virtual 3D world, if you wanted to buy an item that you could use in the virtual realm, you would most likely be using another item of equal worth, such as NFTs or a digital currency, as there were now numerous cryptocurrency companies in existence. As Lincoln explained to Kennedy, "People out there might think that was silly, paying for a fake item with fake money, but the value is often subjective and dictated by supply and demand. How do you think the dollar bills came into existence? They were just pieces of paper with no inherent value until society decided to put a monetary value on them. One day a computer whizz will rally enough of his tech-minded workmates and declare, 'this digital currency is now valuable' and it will be! Is this our calling?

Now Kennedy was right into a fact-finding mission on the metaverse. He realised the idea was of a holistic virtual world that exists in parallel with the real world. "Our whole social connections will change by creating embodied experiences as opposed to just viewing them from a screen," he explained to Lincoln.

They were both excited with what the future held. "Let us just think on this for another week or two and see what ideas we can come up with. Listen to the hype among your financial friends and quiz a bit and I will do the same," Kennedy said.

Life without Reece

Lily's life was back to normal, and she was loving her work. She was now the second-highest qualified lawyer in the law firm, as her qualifications had gained her a career move upwards in the court system. Without Reece at home, she was able to do night classes by correspondence. It was a juggling match with the children, but she still aspired to her dream.

She always found time to fit Kennedy into her busy schedule. It was a distraction from work and a welcome one at that. He had no compunction about staying over at Lily's home for the night, as the marital bed was no more. He had not put any pressure on her to move in, or ask her to come and live with him, as she needed time to herself to sort out her life and move forward.

One morning after a hectic night of love making, Mackenzie walked in on them and asked Kennedy, "Are you our new daddy?" This caught them totally off guard, the truth being he was her rightful birth father. Lily told her, "One day he might be your new daddy. Would you like that?" She tore out of the bedroom yelling, "Harrison, Leila, one day Uncle Kennedy will be our new daddy!" This caused a burst of laughter.

At work one day, Lily was asked to handle a deceased estate as there was a large amount of money involved. The client belonged to another lawyer who had since left the firm, so now it had become Lily's responsibility. Although the deceased was a client of their law firm, he was unknown to Lily, so she would have to familiarise herself with this case. That night she took his file home and spent until the early hours of the morning studying it, to find he had made his money from real estate. She was surprised to find the will did not mention a wife, just a daughter who was the sole beneficiary. As she read on, there was a request for the daughter, Amelia, to find her missing mother and make sure she was financially looked after. The next morning Lily contacted the daughter to come to the office and make herself known, so they could go through a few important details.

Lily met Amelia Harmond, a vibrant young lady, and she guessed she was intelligent and worldly. After the introductions Lily couldn't wait to find out about the missing mother, so she asked Amelia to tell her about her life.

"My mother left my father, me and my brother. She just disappeared, so I believe. I was only six so I don't remember her. In father's last few months, he tried to find her, as he wanted her to know that my brother was tragically killed not long after she left. He lived every day with the pain of losing his son, and it never left him, so he buried himself in work, hence his wealth. I don't know if he felt guilt over what happened, as it was a surprise to me that he wanted to find her. He has requested that I continue to search for her, but I have exhausted all avenues that I know about."

Lily listened to her sad story then asked, "Would you like me to help search for your mother? I know where to go to find the relevant information on missing people." Amelia's eyes lit up, as she had come to a standstill, not knowing what to do next.

Lily asked for any information Amelia could give her regarding dates and names. "I remember my father telling me her name was Lauren and that she had been married before she met him. I don't know who she married before meeting my father. He never talked about her much so that is all I can tell you."

Lily thanked her. "Leave this with me and I'll start a search on Lauren Harmond. Give me a fortnight and hopefully I will be able to bring you some good news." When Amelia left, Lily worked out her age, so now she had a birth year as well as the mother's name. This was a beginning!

It was back to the library to search through the fiches covering births, deaths and marriages. First, she would look for Amelia's birth certificate as it would mention both her father's and mother's names. She looked up the year, then had to go through hundreds of names beginning with 'H'. It was three hours later when she discovered Amelia's birth certificate, but she was shocked to find another birth on the same certificate, that of a boy named Peter! Amelia had not mentioned she was a twin.

Lily looked at her watch and was surprised. Where had the day gone? It was time to pack up and go home. She would come back tomorrow and search the marriages. That night as she lay in bed her mind went back to the day's findings. A feeling of sadness enveloped her. Was there more behind this than met the eye?

After searching alphabetically through the 'H' she eventually found a marriage certificate for a Richard and Lauren Harmond. On the certificate Lily noticed the mother's married name before she married Amelia's father was Barclay. "That name sounds familiar," she muttered to herself. "Lauren Barclay." She kept repeating this name over and over, when suddenly the penny dropped. Barclay, that was Kennedy's surname and his mother's name was Lauren. Was this the missing children that she had walked out on? Had she found Kennedy and Reece's half-sister? Was this wishful thinking or was it the truth? She needed time to think about this new information.

Lily was mystified that Amelia hadn't mentioned that she was a twin. To find out more about the deceased Peter, Lily went to the deaths microfiche to see if she could uncover what might have happened to him. Would the cause be on the death certificate she wondered? She knew the birth date as it was the same as Amelia's. It took a further two hours of searching to find what she was looking for. Peter's death was listed as 'accidental overdose', but he was only seven or thereabouts, so what did this mean? She would ask Amelia what happened when they next met.

As she was driving home, thoughts of what she had discovered haunted Lily. Had she found the other half-sister? If so then the missing mother was dead, and here the search ended! How would Amelia feel to know her mother would have died a pauper if not for Kennedy, especially when there was money available? Lily didn't know what to do next; should she talk it over with Kennedy?

As she pulled into the driveway, there was his car parked at her home and she could see him playing out on the lawn with the children who were yelling and having fun; in fact Kennedy was the biggest kid. While walking past the letter box she saw a large brown envelope sticking out, so she lifted the flap and pulled it out. Yes, it looked like a lawyer's letter, and she knew it was from Reece's lawyer, so she took it inside and put it on the bench to look at later.

After hugging the children and touching Kennedy she went and changed to prepare dinner. Kennedy sat with Leila and listened to her reading as this was her homework. Then he ran a shower for the twins so they would be ready for bed when their bedtime came. He loved sharing the parenting with Lily, which she was so grateful for, as this never happened with Reece. It was only one week before Mackenzie and Harrison started school so they were excited, as they were big kids then.

There was so much going on in Lily's head, but one thing was foremost: she needed to feel Kennedy's arms around her holding her close to his body, then a feeling of intimacy would flow between them.

Once the children were settled for the night, Lily took his hand and led him to the bedroom. When this happened, he knew what was on Lily's mind. She needed him and he would certainly deliver. Once the bedroom door closed, Kennedy wrapped his arms around her, pulling her body close to his, then the warmth radiated between them. His testosterone was running wild, so he lifted her on to the bed and lay beside her, declaring his love for her over and over again, making her feel so special. It was as if he knew what women wanted to hear, but he could only talk this way with Lily, no one else. This is why he stopped dating, hoping one day she would belong to him.

But the wait had been unbearable until that fateful night when he took her without consent. That was the past, now she was his and he had been forgiven. He unbuttoned her blouse and fondled her well-endowed breasts, then his hands slid down her body, caressing her until he touched her womanly parts. Lily's hands were working hard to undo his jeans. She wanted to feel his proud manly membrane and it was there waiting for her. She lifted her body so her knickers could be easily removed. She was ready for him and pleaded that he take her, for him to enter her so they could be joined in body and soul. This was just another of their love-making sessions, with many more to follow.

The next morning as Lily was preparing breakfast she noticed the envelope she had left there yesterday. It had completely slipped her mind, as she had more pleasant things to focus on. She slipped the knife into the envelope and opened it, then began reading. It was as she predicted, a letter from Reece's lawyer laying out how much money he was prepared to share with her and the children. Lily wasn't too concerned as she was making a good return from her investment in the law firm, along with her wages. Then there was Kennedy, who wanted to share his fortune with her and the children. He would give Lily every penny he owned if she asked for it.

It wasn't until the end of the letter that the shock came. Reece wanted sole custody of Leila as her birth father. Lily shed tears as she read this, as no way could she separate the children; they were a family. She would agree to Leila spending the school holidays with him, but certainly not sole custody. She would fight this to the end. Sadly Kennedy had left for work so she couldn't discuss it with him. Then suddenly her thoughts turned to Amelia. She had even forgotten to mention this to Kennedy. Love had overridden all her worries, but for a short while only!

During her lunch hour Lily replied to Reece's lawyer agreeing to all except for the sole custody of Leila. Leila could spend the school holidays with her father, but sole custody she would fight it in court. She made her thoughts clearly known, then gave the letter to her junior clerk to post.

Now her thoughts went back to Amelia, and she wanted to know what happened to Peter, her twin. It was while she was thinking of Peter, she realised that Reece's father's name was Peter, and he was the one Lauren met and fell in love with while working in the department store. Did she love him that much that she named a son after him. How sad? Perhaps she wanted to hold on to memories of their affair, as it must have been a bitter pill to swallow when he walked away.

Today Amelia was meeting with Lily to see if she had found any information on her mother. Ten minutes after she had finished her lunch, Amelia turned up. "Do you have any news for me?" she asked.

"Yes, I do, but, first, why didn't you tell me you and your brother were twins?"

"What do you mean? I always thought my brother was older than me. I was only six when he died so I don't remember very much about him," Amelia replied.

Lily then asked her what had happened to Peter.

"I'm not sure as father never spoke about him, and all I remember is someone swallowed some pills as they thought they were lollies. Perhaps that's what happened."

Lily then went on to explain she had found the birth certificates and they were both born on the same day.

"Father never said we were twins; I wonder why he didn't tell me? Did you find anything on my mother? Perhaps she can tell me more?" she asked.

Lily put her hand across the desk and took Amelia's hand in hers, as she didn't know how she would react to the news she was about to hear. "Your mother has passed away; she is buried here in town. She had a very sad life and if it wasn't for the fact she found her son Kennedy, she would have been buried a pauper."

Tears appeared in her eyes as she asked who Kennedy was. A little story turned into a long one as Lily explained that Kennedy was her half-brother. "But that's not all; you have another half-brother. Your mother had a child out of wedlock who she called Reece, before she married Kennedy's father. They had two children."

"How do you know all this?" Amelia asked.

Lily didn't know where to start, and her life sounded as complicated as Amelia's mother's life. She elected to tell her Kennedy was her partner and he was the father of her twins. It would have been too much to expect her to understand the whole story.

"When can I meet Kennedy?" she enquired.

Lily told her where she lived and she would make sure Kennedy was there when she visited, so they made a date and a time.

"You do have a car?" asked Lily.

Amelia replied with a yes.

The meeting

Today was the meeting of two family members who didn't know each other existed. Lily told Kennedy she had a surprise for him, so he was eager to find out what it was. She decided to wait and see how he would react when meeting his half-sister.

Kennedy arrived first, eager to see what awaited him, only to be told he would have to wait as it hadn't turned up yet. As they were talking, a beautiful red two-door Ferrari pulled up outside Lily's gate.

"My God, look at that car, who does it belong to?" gasped Kennedy.

Poor Lily, she was just as blown away as he was.

Out climbed Amelia. "Hi, Lily," she called as she walked down the driveway towards them. "Hi, you must be Kennedy?" she said as she held out her hand.

Who was this person and how did she know his name?

It was time for Lily to do the introductions. "Kennedy meet your half-sister, Amelia."

He let his hand fall as he stared at this strange young lady. It took a few minutes for it to sink in, then he reached out and invited her into his arms. She clung to him as he was the only remaining family member she had left. From there a conversation began between them, neither wanting to stop asking questions. It was excitement mixed with sadness, but they were both learning about aspects of each other's lives. Lily walked away to let the two of them talk in private.

Once they had caught up on each other's background, they called Lily to come and join them. She brought the children to meet Amelia. "These are the twins Mackenzie and Harrison, and this is Leila."

"Are they your children, Kennedy?" she asked.

"No, our daddy is away in Auckland," piped up Leila. This answer left a blank look on Amelia's face so Lily intervened and whispered, "I will tell you later." Kennedy asked Amelia if she would like to see where their mother was buried.

"Yes please, I'm sad I didn't get to meet her."

Lily decided to stay home with the children so they could have time to grieve together, as the children would be a distraction. She hoped Kennedy might tell Amelia about their relationship, but she would have to wait and see.

As Lily thought about things, she realised Reece hadn't been told about his half-sister, so she decided to call him on his private number.

"Hello, Natalia speaking," was what greeted her. She asked to speak to Reece and was told to hold on. When he eventually spoke, he was polite and asked about the children. She then told him about his half-sister Amelia and her deceased twin brother.

"His name was Peter. Your mother must have named him after your father. Perhaps she never got over him. How is the new hotel going?" she asked.

He told her things were a bit quiet but like any new business, he had to establish himself. "I've decided not to pursue sole custody of Leila, it would not be fair to split the children, so we would love to have her in the holidays. Have you moved in with Kennedy yet?" he asked.

Lily told him she was still on her own, in her own home with the children. "Feel free to come down anytime and meet Amelia," she offered, to which he agreed.

Kennedy and Amelia arrived back from the cemetery several hours later, as he had taken her to his home so they could talk in peace. He had explained his position within the family and talked of his love for Lily. She could understand how awkward it was when they found out they were half-brothers, having both fallen in love with the same lady. Kennedy was happy to know she was financially secure; in fact, she was a very wealthy young lady and they both shared the same thoughts, wishing their mother had found them sooner and shared in their wealth. But sadly, this was not to be.

As soon as the children saw Kennedy, they nabbed him to come outside and play with them, and of course he didn't disappoint. This left Lily and Amelia together, so now was the time for Lily to explain Leila's outspoken comment.

As she began, Amelia silenced her by saying that Kennedy had explained everything to her. "He is a lovely guy, Lily; I hope you will both be happy. Now I know I have family, can I come and visit?" she asked.

"You are most welcome, Amelia. Reece is coming down soon so he will want to meet you. Come to the office on Monday and we will finalise your father's estate, now that we know your mother is deceased."

Virtual reality versus the real world

There it was in the headlines again, 'A popular network platform has been renamed Meta'. Was this so the billionaire could have first slice of the newly named metaverse, which was gaining popularity? Virtual reality and augmented reality were quickly becoming huge areas of technology, with giants like Apple, Microsoft and Google competing to provide the next big experience. Lincoln knew because of his involvement in tech programming, and the large amount of gaming sales, that young users were waiting to be teleported into exciting new experiences. Specially now as there was a demographical shift advancing into the mainstream.

Kennedy and Lincoln knew that with new technologies the virtual world had become far more expansive and convincing, as now the user instead of identifying with the screen could go inside and become whatever or whoever. It allows users near total escapism … building worlds of their dreams where they can be enmeshed for hours, days, months, or in the Minecraft game, for years.

Lincoln could fully understand how this could happen, as since Covid he had isolated himself by working from home, even buying his groceries online. Being the computer nerd that he was, he could immerse himself for hours, forgetting about the outside world. He thought of himself falling victim to virtual reality. With emerging technologies and a world which is more unstable than ever, the virtual world is getting closer to reality as the similarities between the two are closer now than ever before.

With all his up-to-date computer equipment and his knowledge of technology, Lincoln showed Kennedy how users can immerse themselves in a simulated world via hardware, headsets and software. Kennedy was amazed, as he lived in the real world. He could see Lincoln isolating himself and creating his presence in a virtual environment. He was a guy who didn't like making commitments as was his partner; they just came and went to suit themselves. He had no intentions of becoming a family man, which Kennedy couldn't understand, but that was the difference between the real world and the virtual world. He could create a new life in virtual reality, where he was the master of his own destiny.

However, there is one fact that distinguishes the virtual world from the real world and that is the conception of risk, which is not yet fully realised within the virtual world. Lincoln had experienced this, as he was driving the car of his dreams in his virtual world and crashed. He wasn't hurt, he just walked away without so much as a scratch, but if this had happened in the real world, he could have killed himself. He did wonder if he spent a significant amount of time in virtual reality whether he would become addicted and tend to enjoy it there, more than in the real world. Would he eventually become isolated and lose himself from reality? This was his biggest worry. He was a prime candidate and well he knew it, as he lived and breathed technology.

The twins were now at school, and Leila being the big sister took charge of them. She was miss bossy two shoes. She was happy today as her daddy and a lady were coming to visit them, although she didn't know who the lady was.

Lily's last encounter with Natalia was in Reece's suite at the hotel, when she paid him an unexpected visit, so she hoped this meeting was going to be a bit more pleasant. She had arranged for Amelia to come around at 5.30 to meet Reece and have drinks, so she was making a couple of platters.

Kennedy had been invited but declined, as he didn't think it was appropriate for him to join them today, although Amelia thought different, as she wanted both her half-brothers to be there. This was a chance for the children, especially Leila, to meet Natalia, and this would give Lily an insight into how she would interact with children, as she never wanted a family of her own.

Reece and Natalia were staying with Lincoln. As Lily was putting the final touches to the platters the doorbell rang so Leila ran to answer it, and standing there was her daddy. She let out a yell, "Mackenzie and Harrison, Daddy has arrived." Reece bent down and hugged her and before he could do his introductions Leila asked, "Who is this?" Reece was caught off guard and said she was his new partner.

"But what about Mummy?" Leila enquired in an indignant manner. Poor Reece, but Natalia came to his rescue, "You can come and spend holidays with us in Auckland. Would you like that?" she asked.

Leila shrugged her shoulders. "Are you staying with Daddy?" was her next question. Lily intervened and told her not to ask any more questions, that it was rude. As the twins came up to Reece, he just ruffled their hair, and it was then Lily picked up on his off-handedness and felt hurt that he was indifferent to them. None of this was their fault, but she knew he was still hurting over finding out that Kennedy was their biological father.

The silence was broken by another door knock and in walked Amelia. "Amelia, this is Reece and his partner Natalia," said Lily as she introduced them.

"Hi, Reece, it is lovely to meet you. I am so happy to know that I still have family," and with this he held out his hand. Amelia took the initiative and gave him a hug. Once conversation got underway, there was no stopping them as they had plenty to catch up on.

Lily invited Natalia to come and have a glass of wine and some nibbles in the dining room where the children were playing. Mackenzie asked Natalia if she wanted to play, but she declined. Lily could see she wasn't a hands-on person with children, as Leila had parked herself next to her hoping for some attention, but when it wasn't forthcoming, she moved away.

Lily asked her about the hotel and Natalia talked a little about it.

"Reece told me you are in the legal profession; you must be clever?" she asked. Lily explained her years at university and her night classes to get more credits so she could pursue her dream to be a High Court judge. Then the conversation veered away to Amelia and her relationship to Reece and Kennedy. All the time the children were coming up to the table and helping themselves to nibbles and, still, Natalia didn't converse with them.

Lily and Natalia had nearly polished off a bottle of wine by the time Reece and Amelia joined them. Reece was surprised to know that Amelia's twin brother was named Peter. He wondered if, as Lily had mentioned, his mother had never forgotten his father. This was the only bit of joy he felt about his biological parents. He never allowed himself to feel much affection for them as he loved his adoptive parents; they were his family. Another bottle of wine was produced and conversations flowed.

Amelia asked if Reece and Kennedy could visit the cemetery tomorrow with her together and say a prayer for their mother. Reece agreed, so she told him she would pick up Kennedy and they would meet at the cemetery gates. "Natalia and I will take the children to the playground while you guys do your thing. Is that okay with you?" she asked.

Natalia nodded her head in reply. 'This will be a test,' Lily thought to herself.

Amelia arrived at Kennedy's to pick him up in her Ferrari. She had called into a florist and bought a beautiful bouquet of flowers to place on the grave. "Will you and Reece be okay with each other today?" she asked. She found Kennedy so easy to get on with, but Reece was more reserved, so she could see why Lily loved Kennedy.

"Reece and I go back to our university days. We have been friends for years, then when we found out about our family connection things changed a little. But if not for him, Lincoln and I would not be where we are today. It is sad that we both loved the same woman, but Lily and Reece had drifted apart and when I told him the twins were mine, we exchanged blows. It was hard for him to learn the truth but it had to be told. Our friendship will never end. We have come so far together that it will be okay," he assured her.

As they pulled up at the cemetery Reece was already there. Amelia alighted and picked up the flowers. "Hi Reece," she called. They both walked towards him, then Kennedy extended his hand and Reece shook it. They walked to the grave and Amelia laid the flowers at the foot of the headstone. She stood up and asked them to join hands while she prayed. After she finished Kennedy told her that their mother was not alone, as his father had requested to be buried with her to keep her safe. This brought on a flood of tears from Amelia, just to know her mother would have company forever, that her wretched life was now well behind her.

· · ·

Reece and Natalia were leaving to fly back to Auckland. Lily brought the children to the airport so they could say goodbye and was sad to see Reece's indifference to the twins. Leila received a hug while the twins were told 'goodbye'. She knew from that moment that's where Reece's feelings for Mackenzie and Harrison more or less ended. She felt it didn't have to be like that, as they still looked upon him as their father. It left her feeling cold towards him and she was happy that he was now less connected to them as a family.

Natalia seemed well suited to Reece as she was not at all child minded. This she had seen for herself during her visit, and she did wonder how they would manage when Leila went to stay with them, but only time would tell!

That night, Lily's home would be back to normal as Kennedy's presence was sorely missed by her and the children. She had invited him around for dinner and to stay the night, as she needed to feel his body close to hers, so she enticed him with the promise of a roast meal. She knew the way to a man's heart was through his stomach, although Kennedy's heart belonged to Lily totally. This was just an excuse, but she liked to make him feel special, to return those wonderful feelings he shared with her, as they built up her self-esteem, which allowed her to follow her dream. He understood what it meant to Lily to reach her goal. This was what she talked about back in their university quiz days, and she had never faltered. Kennedy admired her tenacity as she had mixed family life with ambition, a tall order, and Lily had honoured both. It was when Reece told him that Lily had to give up her dream and be a full-time mother that he saw red, and the truth came out about the twins. He could not hold back when criticism was made against Lily.

As soon as Kennedy's car pulled up the driveway the children were out like a flash, to nab him to play with them, which allowed Lily to attend to dinner. At the table the atmosphere was so different to when Reece was there, as he couldn't stand the continual chatter of the children, whereas Kennedy encouraged them to talk about their day's schooling. The atmosphere was that of a normal family. Had Lily noticed what it could be like, had she thought more about the family situation lately, was she ready to make another commitment? Once the children were showered and ready for bed, it was story time and Kennedy was asked to do the honours.

At last peace reigned, and now it was time for the adults. "You know, Kennedy, I am so glad Reece has gone. I have very little affection for him, and he is not the man I fell in love with. He has changed. He was out to prove himself, but he didn't need to, as we all liked him as he was, not who he has become," sighed Lily.

"I think it became apparent when he found out his biological father was just a staff member in a department store – that was the final straw," said Kennedy. "It is sad to think that he inherited great wealth and still felt he had to prove himself, but he will always have a part of my heart as he shared his good fortune, which helped make Lincoln and me who we are today. Now that he owns his own hotel, perhaps he will come to terms with himself and find the happiness he is seeking."

"Enough about the past. Let's make the present memorable. Come to bed," beckoned Lily.

He didn't need any encouragement, as he jumped up and lifted her into his arms and carried her through to the bedroom. There the adult games began. Lily asked Kennedy to undress her then she would do the same to him. She wasn't shy with him. He loved her body; it wasn't perfect, but he didn't do perfect when it came to Lily, as she was the mother of his children. Kennedy, on the other hand, she thought was the perfect man, and he owned a well-endowed body, but strangely she was the only person that his body would perform for, as she had a special warmth that flowed through to his heart.

He had no fear of disappointing her, as she could stir the passion needed to send the blood flowing through his body to the very place it needed to go. She loved the effect she had on him, and it allowed her to tease him and play games. But, in the end, it was she who did the begging to be taken, and he was in control, while she definitely was not. For them to become as one was the most wonderful feeling of intimacy, something she only learnt since making love with Kennedy, as his tender words turned her to jelly, and she simply melted.

Kennedy and Lincoln were meeting in Lincoln's high-tech computer room, to further discuss their finances and what investments they were intending to pursue. They had struck the bitcoin and the NFTs as they were on the rise, and in fact they had reached the pinnacle of success and were now millionaires, who were ready to do it all over again, but with what?

Lincoln was the man to investigate, and he came up with a new investment idea, something that was in its early stages, a new playground, that of the metaverse which had come up for investigation a few weeks before. This was taking the interest of Facebook, Amazon and Epic, the maker of the popular game 'Fortnite', a digital world where people could shop till they drop without hurting the planet. Lincoln's hours of study led him to this, as he could see virtual reality would become the next generation of the internet … a second life!

"This is going to turn into a race between the tech giants, and the first to get there will set the boundaries for the ones that follow," stated a convincing Lincoln. This advance in technology sent shivers through his body and he became excited, as this was where his heart lay. Was he becoming obsessed? He knew those who were creators would be the leaders.

He considered that the metaverse would protect the planet through the substitution of physical goods by digital ones, replacing real-world presence with virtual interactions. By doing this it would lessen time or inclination to indulge in more carbon-intensive activities. I can see the metaverse becoming a huge source of joy where I can meet with virtual friends, who would feel like real friends, and I would never be lonely if more lockdowns follow, he thought.

Kennedy listened with interest, but was his friend becoming paranoid about the outside world? Although there had been much talk about the pandemic, was it happening for a reason? It had lowered the number of people travelling for pleasure and for business, which had a flow-on effect that would see a decrease in fuel consumption and air pollution.

"Don't you think the majority of people would happily accept the cheaper option of business meetings from their home, through the metaverse, if it meant keeping safe?" asked Lincoln.

Kennedy needed to churn this over. What did he really think? He was a more practical person. Their brains were wired differently, and his happiness was in the real world. Could Lincoln find the same happiness in the virtual world? Perhaps he could!

As they delved further into for and against, Kennedy was surprised to learn that investors were buying land in the virtual world. "Why would they be doing that?" he asked.

Lincoln pointed out that over $700 million had been spent on virtual land deals in the metaverse to build 3D homes for their avatars to live in. "They are purchasing land with Mana tokens to build art galleries and casinos, along with creating a new virtual city. It is so exciting, I'm going to buy land in the metaverse, as that will be the next big money-spinner. At the moment the land is selling for $20 US per acre. It will take a few years to fully develop but I am prepared to wait. I am young, so are you, Kennedy. Will you come on board?"

"I will talk it over with Lily as she is my love and I have the children to consider. Give me a week and I will get back to you," he told Lincoln. Deep down he knew he could put his trust in Lincoln as he was right up there in the computer world. Computer programmers saw things ahead of the average person. They knew what games were selling and how the younger generation chose to spend their time, so the pathway was clear to them in what direction technology was heading.

When Kennedy spoke with Lily about investing in the metaverse, she told him to do what he felt was right as it was his money, and she didn't want to influence him in any way. She felt it wasn't her position to say where he spent his money. Was now the time to ask Lily to become his partner, as he wanted to share everything he owned with her and the children? Perhaps this would start the ball rolling on divorce proceedings, as he wanted Lily to be his forever love. He knew she had an agenda, and he would encourage her to pursue it.

Lily's dream

Today Lily was asked to attend a meeting as a representative of their legal firm. She had no idea what was going to be discussed and was surprised on her arrival to see a panel of people sitting at a long table. Apart from these people there was no one else in sight, so she felt a little intimidated but was asked to be seated.

The silence was broken. "We are here today to ask if you have a good knowledge of the law and what justice means in present-day New Zealand." Lily was taken aback by this question, but she told herself to keep calm and then her mind could focus on what she had been asked. She didn't disappoint as she was studying at nights, so things were fresh in her mind, so she gave a creditable answer.

She still did not know why she was here today. "Lily, your firm has nominated you for the position of a District

Court Judge. We have a vacancy and they thought you were the right candidate. All we had to do was meet you and ask a few questions. We know you have your Bachelor of Laws degree and have completed a professional Legal Studies course and are a partner in a law firm. If you could leave us for ten minutes then return, we will have made our decision."

Her firm had kept all this secret from her. They knew of her aspirations and if she was lucky enough to get this position, she was well on her way to move up the ranks in the court system. The District Court was the beginning, then came the High Court, after which followed the Court of Appeal and the highest court, the Supreme Court. The waiting played on Lily's mind. Did she do enough? she wondered.

Her concentration was broken by someone asking her to come back into the interview room. "Welcome back, Lily, we have made our decision. Congratulations, the position is yours. We are satisfied that you are the right person and we know you will see justice is done fairly. As from the first of March you can begin the transition to take up your new appointment as a District Court Judge."

Lily thanked the panel and shook their hands. Excitement was bubbling up inside her. She wanted to shout from the tree-tops so everyone could hear her! But first stop was the office, first she would scold her co-workers, then thank them for this opportunity of a lifetime that they had recommended her for.

While at her office Lily fossicked until she found the book containing rules and regulations expected of judges.

She was amazed to learn the jurisdiction of a District Court Judge. It was the widest of all judicial appointments. It involved a wide spectrum of civil and family law cases, claims for damages and injunctions, mortgage borrowers, property tenants, divorce, domestic violence, committal and insolvency proceedings. This took her mind back to the times she had represented clients in court, how her feelings had to be put aside and facts were what a case was built on. It stirred excitement in her belly, and she knew in those moments it was definitely her calling.

Now it was time to leave her workplace and head home to her children. Once they were settled, she would call Kennedy to come over so they could celebrate. First there would be a glass or two of wine followed by an invitation to her boudoir, where the pleasures would begin, pleasures that only he could provide!

Leila's life was full of adventure as she was leaving the next day to fly to Auckland to spend the school holidays with her father. Tonight, there were celebrations and Kennedy and Amelia were invited. A fond friendship had evolved between Leila and Amelia. They all played games and everyone was happy, apart from Lily, as she worried how Leila and Natalia would get on together. But there was nothing she could do as she had agreed to let Reece have her for the holidays. A flight attendant had been arranged to be her chaperone for the flight and to see she was picked up at the Auckland end, presumably by Reece.

Lily cried as she handed Leila over to the flight attendant at the airport. "Don't cry, Mummy, I'm going to have a holiday with Daddy," were her parting words. Lily stood and waved as Leila disappeared hand in hand with her charge. Reece had promised to ring her as soon as she touched down to let her know she had arrived safely. Lily played with the twins to keep her mind occupied, but after three hours of waiting and still no news from Reece, she decided to call him.

Reece was dreading this call. What was he going to tell Lily? He had sent Natalia to the airport to pick up Leila, but she was stuck in traffic so arrived late, only to find that someone else had collected her. A complete stranger had claimed the little girl … but who?

Also by Margaret Nyhon

COMING SOON

The Stolen Girl (sequel to *Fortune Smiles as Love Divides*)

FICTION

Isobella (Book 1 in the *Isobella* series)

Isobella: Self Redemption (Book 2 in the *Isobella* series)

Papa's Girl Emmeline

Betrayal by an Irish Rose

Revenge for an English Lord (sequel to *Betrayal by an Irish Rose*)

For Girls' Eyes Only

Daughters Lost to the Underworld

Pimchan and Amira

Coronavirus: A Novel

The Whistle-blower's Severed Link (sequel to *Coronavirus: A Novel*)

NON-FICTION

de Marisco

Freedom Knows No Boundaries

A Wake-up Call

A Shattered Dream Across the Tasman

Memories and Moving On

About the Author

Margaret Nyhon lives in Mosgiel, New Zealand, where she writes, paints and practises the crafts of printing and bookbinding.

She has worked extensively in hospitality management in New Zealand and resort management in Australia. The urge to trace her family history led her to the writing of her first non-fiction work, *de Marisco*. She has since written several fiction and non-fiction works. Margaret is married and has three adult children and two grandsons.

Contact Margaret: margaretf@hotmail.co.nz